TELL

Totally Amazing Little Exciting Stories

UK Fiction Vol I
Edited by Lynsey Hawkins

Disclaimer

Young Writers has maintained every effort
to publish stories that will not cause offence.

Any stories, events or activities relating to individuals
should be read as fictional pieces and not construed
as real-life character portrayal.

 Young**Writers**

First published in Great Britain in 2006 by:
Young Writers
Remus House
Coltsfoot Drive
Peterborough
PE2 9JX
Telephone: 01733 890066
Website: www.youngwriters.co.uk

SB ISBN 1 84602 659 8

Foreword

Young Writers was established in 1991 and has been passionately devoted to the promotion of reading and writing in children and young adults ever since. The quest continues today. *Young Writers* remains as committed to engendering the fostering of burgeoning poetic and literary talent as ever.

This year, *Young Writers* are happy to present a dynamic and entertaining new selection of the best creative writing from a talented and diverse cross-section of some of the most accomplished secondary school writers around. Entrants were presented with four inspirational and challenging themes.

'Myths And Legends' gave pupils the opportunity to adapt long-established tales from mythology (whether Greek, Roman, Arthurian or more conventional eg The Loch Ness monster) to their own style.

'A Day In The Life Of ...' offered pupils the chance to depict twenty-four hours in the lives of literally anyone they could imagine. A hugely imaginative wealth of entries were received encompassing days in the lives of everyone from the top media celebrities to historical figures like Henry VIII or a typical soldier from the First World War.

Finally 'Short Stories', in contrast, offered no limit other than the author's own imagination! 'Ghost Stories' challenged pupils to write an old-fashioned ghost story, relying on suspense, tension and terror rather than using violence and gore.

Telling T.A.L.E.S. UK Fiction Vol I is ultimately a collection we feel sure you will love, featuring as it does the work of the best young authors writing today.

Contents

Jessica Clancy (12)   29
Michael Aston (12)   30

St Michael's Catholic High School, Watford
Nicholas Adams (12)   31
Louise Leahy (11)   32
Corey Clarke (12)   33
Rosie Moneypenny (13)   34
Denise Flannery (12)   35
Shannon Flaherty (12)   36
Gina Wigg (11)   37
Connor Welch (11)   38
Sam O'Shea (13)   39
Nicole Rixon (13)   40
Paloma Watson (12)   41
Joshua Melsome (12)   42
Lily Hattingh (12)   43
Sherilyn Harding (12)   44
Emily Butcher (11)   45
Adele Rayner (12)   46
Ciara Stewart (12)   47
Regan Kerr (11)   48
Sean Beasley (13)   49
Abbie Slade (12)   50
Paige Coster (12)   51
Ellen Dorrian (12)   52
Louis French (12)   53
Sophie Waller (12)   54
Freya Bartrand (12)   55
Adam McPhail (11)   56
Laura Stanbrook (12)   57
Kieran Kelly (12)   58
Haddy Gibril (12)   59
Georgia Mays (11)   60
Katherine Vovrosh (13)   61
Bradley Bennett (13)   62
Ben Young (12)   63
Kyle Connolly (11)   64
Charlotte Dormon (11)   65
Hannah Whitear (11)   66
Helen Byrne (12)   67

Sean Gower (12)	68
Georgia Barnett (11)	69
Tom Panayiotou (12)	70
Vanessa Nolan (12)	71
Edward Daniels (12)	72
Jason Burge (12)	73
Olivia Squires (12)	74
Tashauna Halligan (12)	75
Jack Townsend (12)	76
Katie Ross (12)	77
Michael Mottershead (11)	78
Chloe O'Sullivan (12)	79
Conor Carney (12)	80
Marisa Scannell (12)	81
Eleanor Nutkins (12)	82
Jessica Fuller (12)	83
Amy Lovell (12)	84
Geneva Mayuga (11)	85
Brodie O'Shea (12)	86
Fiona Burke (12)	87
Kyle Quayc (11)	88
Amy Jenkins (13)	89
Erin Oakley (13)	90
Laura Graham (13)	91
Sean McNally	92
Nathan Dunton (12)	93
Luisa Beeken (13)	94
Tasha Msanide (13)	95
Michael O'Toole (12)	96
Jack Dorgan (11)	97
Heidi Currid (12)	98
Charlotte Gomez (12)	99
Danielle McAuley (15)	100
Abbi-Louise Wright (15)	102
Charlotte Parker (14)	103
Aisling Carney (15)	104
Jade Cook	105
Stefania Zeoli	106
Sarah Loughran (15)	107
Liam Maguire (11)	108
Kalisha Ketchen (11)	109
Lucy Dunne (12)	110

The Creative Writing

A Day In The Life Of Darcey Bussell

I stood backstage, my heart beating so fast, I wondered if I was still alive! The lights went down, the curtains up and the music started. I had been rehearsing for so long, maybe too long; maybe it was too hard as I seemed not to remember any of my dance. I had to do it. I watched two dancers run on, to start their ballet duet. I got into my starting position, and waited for my cue. I saw the two dancers come off, red in the face, panting, but also giggling and smiling at the same time. *They had done it, surely I can do it too?* I thought to myself, trying to reassure myself. The music got louder, it was my time to shine!

I ran on stage. The audience was dark, but there was a bright spotlight pointing straight at me. I leapt into a pirouette, I danced wonderfully, turning and pirouetting beautifully, finally I finished. I felt spectacular, I had had butterflies in my stomach, but now I was just in a whirl! I heard the audience clapping. I had done it!

I ran back on stage and did my bow. Flowers were thrown at me. I looked around, all the dancers surrounded me, also clapping and cheering. I couldn't believe it! There was nothing to describe how incredible I felt!

Lydia Arnoux (13)
Abbots Bromley School for Girls, Rugeley

A Day In The Life Of Pippa Funnel

I awoke to the sound of Supreme Rock's whinny. I got up not knowing how we would tackle the grand badminton event. At 6am in the morning I was ready for what would be thrown our way.

Supreme Rock was loaded into the horsebox; my mum wished me luck as we set off.

The Badminton show grounds were packed with people and horses; I steadily unloaded Supreme Rock and tied him up with a haynet. This was it, time to enter. 'No going back now Pippa' I remembered my mum say. I was handed a number and bought a coffee.

As I pulled the bridle over Supreme Rock's head, he looked at me as if to say everything would be OK. I knew my horse well, I had no option but to trust him.

We eyed the competition against us; my good friend spotted me and wished me luck. Time to warm up.

Supreme Rock was going well, transitions were good and not a fault could I put against his jumping. My name was shouted to enter the collecting ring; we were competing in just under ten minutes time.

The bell rang as the present competitor was led out of elimination. My name was called, as papers were organised I glared at each fence and gave Supreme Rock the same opportunity. Then I heard the bell. I approached the first huge fence ... one ... two ... three ...

Lauren Bromley (13)
Abbots Bromley School for Girls, Rugeley

A Day In The Life Of Max

Hi my name's Max and I'm eight years old, and, in High Hope Orphanage. I have been here since I was three days old. My best friend's name is Adam and he's 8 too. Adam and I always play football together in the playground with the ball Adam's nan gave him. She is really old and can't look after Adam so he's in the orphanage with me.

Today we had what the orphanage like to call 'Collection Day' and once again, I was not picked by anyone! I don't know why but they all seem to say 'what a shame'. I told Barry, the guy who looks after all the children on the H for Happy Ward. He says that it is because I am special in my own way, and that if he was looking for a child he would have me. Unfortunately, he isn't looking for a kid.

We are now going for dinner to see who has and hasn't been picked. I will be back in about 15 minutes.

Adam has gone, my best friend. I don't know what to do. I don't have anyone, even just at dinner I didn't have anybody to talk to. I can't believe he left without saying goodbye. I will be all alone with nobody to hug or to snuggle up to when I am sad. Adam might have just been given a cuddle with adults, not by me. Please if you see Adam, tell him I miss him!

Faye Carrington (13)
Abbots Bromley School for Girls, Rugeley

The End Of The Line

'Devon … Devon!'

Devon stopped suddenly on the upstairs landing. Who was calling him? Blaming his imagination, he entered his bedroom; but then he heard the voice again. It was telling him to go outside. Devon couldn't control his curiosity and obeyed the haunting voice. He reached the front door only to hear the whisper, 'Follow my voice Devon, follow.'

He seemed to be in a trance, he couldn't control his body, he just wanted to break free! He walked down the cold driveway heading for the train station which was exactly where his body took him. He clambered down some steep steps onto the railway, but he felt so weak and just collapsed onto the dirty ground. He crawled around and when he reached the metal tracks, he just lay there, paralysed. He was struggling to keep his eyes open, when he felt compression against his chest. With the little strength he could conjure, he felt rough rope, slowly being tied around his body. What was happening?

'Your time is up. Goodbye Devon,' whispered the unfriendly voice.

'What do you mean?' he asked, alarmed.

Then his ears heard a faint bell from down the track … a train! Devon struggled and struggled but the rope held him tight. He was panicking but couldn't scream!

Then everything went black. Devon opened his eyes into a squint and he could see grey panels, the same colour as his bedroom ceiling! He thought he must have been dreaming … but why could he still hear the train?

Olivia Dodd (13)
Abbots Bromley School for Girls, Rugeley

Alea Tonga

My name is Alea Tonga, I live in Outer Nebarondo, this is my life. I was always happy as a child and complained about my life. In the morning I would go and fetch water, I would then come home and help my mother cook and boil the water. After I would feed my little sister Carna, the most beautiful baby, although she was very thin. I never knew my father, he died before Carna was born, before that he was kept in one of the only two rooms we had. I was never allowed to see him.

My family were probably one of the poorest in our village, but no one treated us differently for it. Everyone tried to help out and things weren't that bad. Then things had a turn for the worse, that summer my mama fell ill. Mama still tried to work but I knew it hurt her and one day she just collapsed. I was so scared, my heard was racing and I just belted down into the village to get help, but no one came, no one cared. I staggered back, feeling like the weight of the world was on my shoulders and no one would relieve me.

When I returned Mama was still on the floor in pain but with open eyes. Carna was crying, I picked her up and then laid a blanket around Mama.

In the morning I woke and turned to Mama. I went to kiss her, her cheek was cold. I felt her pulse. Carna and I were all alone.

Eve Fehilly (13)
Abbots Bromley School for Girls, Rugeley

A Day In The Life Of A Wardrobe

Do you want to know something interesting? Yes? I have many stories to tell, one including how a girl called Vikki's parents were murdered.

Vikki's mum was a housewife. Her dad had lost his job, so money became scarce. He turned to betting, and soon no money was left. He couldn't pay the bookies their money, then one day they came to their house.

They arrived at noon. Vikki's dad took them upstairs, she stood inside the wardrobe. He whispered, 'Daddy loves you,' and kissed her.

Vikki peered through a gap, panic resounding through her. The footsteps became heavier matching her pulse, anxiety smothered the room. Silence abruptly fell as the footsteps stopped. A devious-looking man slid into the room, two bigger men followed. They immediately went to Vikki's dad and threw him against the wall. 'This business is not a joke.' Vikki watched in trepidation as they beat her dad, her mother huddled in the corner kicked by the third man.

Tears engulfed her face and dripped down her hands. Her parents slipping away, she tried to recall happier times. Two gunshots ended the massacre. Silence entered the room as the men left. 'Mum, Dad?' Vikki gently pushed the door open, she knelt down next to them. Their blood seeping into the carpet, and staining her skin. She became numb, happiness leaked out of her. One tear crawled down her face and drowned in her parents' blood.

Only Vikki knew the truth. Objects know more than what meets the eye.

Liyin Yip (13)
Abbots Bromley School for Girls, Rugeley

Handbag Queen

I'm bored of sitting on this shelf, me £2,000 and only 44 people in my three years of being a handbag at Dior. Only 44 people have ever picked me up to observe. So today I got promoted to the middle of the shop on the best stand, with my matching shoes. Let's see what happens.

Oh my goodness, it has only been days and Britain's best model, Kerry, has bought me and my matching shoes. We are going to Spain tomorrow on an aeroplane, how exciting.

The time has come, I have my make-up inside me and we're off to the airport. I'm going to have go in the luggage section on the aeroplane.

I don't like it. I fall asleep but get woken by a lady who is fumbling inside me. She realises I am not hers. Then she takes me to a desk where a horrible man is waiting to get his grubby hands on me. He puts me on a shelf with lots of distressed bags.

I get chatting with a very handsome suit bag next to me, he's been here a year. I stop and think. *What if Kerry never comes back, what do I do then?* No one to spill their foundation in me and no one to put me away, so I don't get dirty. Hang on I can hear a familiar *click, click* of heels, there's my matching shoes. Kerry's here to pick me up!

Maddy Moore (13)
Abbots Bromley School for Girls, Rugeley

A Day In The Life Of A Door

Here today I tell you of my life and what I saw. A stocky man with five o'clock shadow bought me and this is my first memory. I was soon to find out that I would hang on a girl of about 14's hinges called Eve. She was a kind and considerate girl that only slammed me once and this is it.

It was a normal sunny day and she was getting ready for a date. It was 7 o'clock and her dad had been drinking again. He came up to her room and told her that she could not go.

She asked him why, but no answer came. He walked away staring at her. In her fury she slammed the door at his malicious smile and hit him on his long pointy nose. He staggered back and a thud was heard. He'd tumbled down the stairs.

Eve was in her room climbing out of the window, when she heard the thud and she looked at what she had done. She called the ambulance and they took him to hospital. There wasn't much blood but there was a splodge on me.

It turned out he was OK and no serious harm was done. She never slammed me again and ended up marrying the guy she saw that night, but her father never liked him. There is still a mark on me where she slammed me, but now I'm old and weary and no longer care.

Emily Paddock (13)
Abbots Bromley School for Girls, Rugeley

The Murder That Never Was

Bang! Then stunned silence. That was the day I was murdered.

It was in July, I woke up to find it was a sizzling day. Everyone was very lethargic because it was so hot. I decided to go for a walk. I remember a man in front of me, his face seemed familiar, he was with a girl, a very pretty girl, she had golden hair. He seemed agitated, his eyes looked furtively. He said something to the girl, I couldn't quite hear, but it was something to do with money. Suddenly he turned around and looked at me straight in the eye and, even though it was a warm day, I felt a cold shiver down my spine, then suddenly they were gone.

Had she heard what I'd said? When I turned to look at her I had a feeling she knew. I couldn't take a chance now, I'm not going to prison not for anyone especially not for her. I told Betty I had to go and meet a friend but I followed Miss Nosy out of the park. She stopped at the library, I couldn't go in so I hovered around the entrance. I hoped I wasn't seen or my face recognised from the wanted poster. As she left I followed her, my heart was pounding faster and faster. I took the gun from my pocket and I knew what I had to do! Bang! I pulled the trigger.

Verity Robb (13)
Abbots Bromley School for Girls, Rugeley

The Smiths

There were some new residents in the village of Lyme, they were as dark as the night and as mysterious as a lake which you cannot see the end of because the fog is hiding it.

There was a shed right on the outskirts which looked as if it had just been hit by a hurricane. An old man lived there, he was called Mr Riley, his mother and father had died when he was young and after that people said he was mad.

A tradition for the village was to have a party for any new residents. It was time for the party, everyone was there, the new residents who called themselves the Smiths looked very pale, didn't talk much, they wouldn't eat or drink and stayed in the same place for the whole party. When Mr Riley came in he froze, went as white as a ghost, the whole room was silent. He pointed his finger at the Smiths, it was shaking. He shouted, 'Mum, Dad.' Everyone started laughing, they thought he was mad.

The party ended, the Smiths invited Mr Riley upstairs. He noticed they had no feet and were hovering. He ran for the door, then there was a high-pitched scream, two spirits were circling around him, they had dropped the flesh and bones of his parents. They climbed into Mr Riley's body, and ever since that day people say he has three personalities.

Beth Serougi (13)
Abbots Bromley School for Girls, Rugeley

A Day In The Life Of Annabelle

Her eyes peered through the keyhole like clear slate pools, seeing that the coast was clear she opened the door no more than five centimetres so she could fit her scrawny little body through, effortless, then she ran into the corridor, her long chestnut hair waved like a luscious foreign waterfall. Her footsteps were silent as the rest of the house. She reached the staircase, she gasped at the sight of these ghastly stairs. Their old dark wood groaned like a prisoner at every step. She closed her eyes, she ran her hand down the banister, her feet followed.

Three floors down she reached the basement and took a breath of relief, her eyes became sharp and aware again. A shadow appeared at the door to the kitchen and it was getting bigger. Her eyes widened, she dashed behind five crates of bread. The chef was a plump man who smelled of chilli and tea leaves. He had coarse black hair and sharp small eyes. He was not a hygienic man as he often wiped his nose on the back of his hand. He removed the top crate and went to his kitchen like a badger to its sett. She made a run for it as soon as his shadow disappeared. She leapt down the corridor. This wasn't wise. She felt a greasy hand cling to her arm; she managed to get out of his clasp, only to be swallowed by the fearful darkness.

Kimberley Simmons (12)
Abbots Bromley School for Girls, Rugeley

The End To A Perfect Day

The clear water ripples as we step into the shining new speedboat, the sun scorching hot as it beats down on our backs. I look round with my hands over my eyes, shielding them from the bright rays. No clouds in the sky; a perfect day in Hawaii.

We launch away from the golden beach and out into the ocean. The wind blows my long hair out of my face, cooling us from the heat of the sun. I observe the view - pure paradise. We see the shore that we've left behind us, in the distance, along with the white foamy waves we've created from the boat. Up ahead, I can see an island with a beach similar to the one we just left. Over the purr of the engine, my dad shouts, 'Shall we stop there to eat?'

I say yes and he gently docks the boat.

We decide to eat in the shade, and then explore the island. I spot some coconuts up in the green leaves of a tree and am about to climb up it when I hear a threatening *crunch* and I spin to the direction of the sound. I run to it and find a tangled mess where the boat had been, slowly sinking, along with the emergency kit and phone. Dad halts beside me, and points into the distance, where I unmistakeably see - a silver fin. I look out into my perfect day and realise ... I guess you could say we were shipwrecked.

Hannah Watkins (12)
Abbots Bromley School for Girls, Rugeley

A Day In The Life Of A Lioness

The glistening water rippled as the beautiful lioness gently stroked the water with her tongue. Her paws gripped the hard, dusty ground, raising her amazing powerful body that was covered in gorgeous golden fur sweating in the heat of the morning sun.

The creature slowly lifted her head out of the pool, gracefully made her way up the hill and pounded on relentlessly. Silently she continued onto her den. When she arrived her suspicions were raised. There was no sound of her cute cubs that she had safely left just an hour ago! Her heart beat faster and faster as she continued down the labyrinth to the centre of the well-constructed den.

She arrived at the den's centre, not only to find her four helpless cubs missing, but also the footprints of the guilty party all around, hyenas. She rushed from the maze and raced along, sniffing the air for her enemy. The wise, magnificent lioness knew the exact location of the predators' home. Within an hour she was within hearing distance of her quarry.

She walked on keeping low so that she was hidden in the long dry grasses. Eventually she reached her destination. The mere thought of the hyenas was beginning to poison her mind.

The lioness entered the dank cave keeping in the shadows, as if invisible. Then she saw them. Her cubs! Huddled together like pieces of a jigsaw caged behind an ugly, bloodthirsty hyena. She pounced and the hyena's last breath was drawn.

Hannah Thomas (13)
Abbots Bromley School for Girls, Rugeley

The Vampire Bites Back

I will never forget the time I first laid eyes on her. That morning on New Year's Eve one hundred years ago now, I had split up with my girlfriend. I knew it would never last.

That night at a New Year party, I saw her. I was finding the party quite mundane. I started to leave, she appeared. Her hypnotic blue eyes glistened as they wandered about the room, her radiant porcelain skin, luscious ruby-red lips, and her long black hair shining in the moonlight. She was so beautiful standing there so statuesque, like a goddess. I wanted to be with her forever. Our eyes met and locked, she was in my head, I walked over to her in an uncontrollable daze, a voice chanting in my head leading me, towards her. We danced, we glided across the floor, the floor was ours.

On the stroke of midnight we kissed, there was an intense piercing pain at the side of my neck. I heard chanting in my head, the room was racing around me, I felt my blood drain out of my body, but I could not understand why I was still conscious while my heart had stopped. Pictures were flashing through my mind of events of the past, present and future. A strange wave of consciousness and a new understanding of the world came over me, as I kissed Katrina's bloodstained lips, and with this the peace of knowing we would be together for all of eternity.

Brittany Stafford (13)
Abbots Bromley School for Girls, Rugeley

The End

The sirens were wailing all around us. As soon as the first siren had sounded panic struck. 'Gas masks on!' the teacher shouted above the noise, at the same time struggling to get her own mask fixed on her face.

We all did as we were told and I picked up my gas mask, my hands shaking. We formed an orderly line and rushed out of the classroom.

By the time we reached the hall everyone was running frantically. I heard someone screaming, 'They're here, the Germans are here!' and a bright light shone in my eyes.

Then I heard it, and for a split second nothing happened. All at once the walls started crumbling in and screams rang through my ears. The engine of a German aircraft roared overhead. Through the dust I saw a beam of light and I ran towards it; I ran as fast as I could just longing to reach the light, just longing to live.

Time seemed to stand still as I yearned to be free. I dodged around people and falling bricks, but finally I reached the gap in the rubble where the light was streaming through, now all I need is to thrust my arm through there ...

Suddenly my eardrums were shattered by another loud explosion followed immediately by another, and another. We were now under full scale attack, little children were wailing beside me. One more bomb fell and all around me the walls shook. Then before I could blink they tumbled in on me, I looked up barely able to move. Dust fell into my eyes, then everything went black ...

Karris Hamilton (12)
Friargate House School, Derby

The Minotaur

We were under King Minos' gloomy, dark castle in the labyrinth where the Minotaur was kept. My mission was to slay it.

Before I entered the labyrinth I had set eyes on the king's daughter, Princess Ariadne, and we immediately fell in love with one another. She handed me a sword and a long roll of thread which I now kept under my cloak. I told my scared and helpless companions to wait at the entrance while I went to confront the monstrous beast. I tied one end of the thread to my belt and the other end to the door and set off to make my way through the labyrinth. Its never-ending paths branched and branched again perplexingly. Until, what seemed like hours of walking, I turned a corner and I could see a dark and beastly shadow and could also hear the heavy breathing of the Minotaur as I entered his lair, it turned around and noticed me. He charged at me violently. In a moment our arms were locked in a deadly struggle. I managed to lay my hand on the hilt of the sword Ariadne had given me, with one superhuman effort I managed to slice off the creature's head.

I picked up the head with triumph and headed back to the entrance by following the thread which Ariadne had also given me.

Phil Wright (14)
Friargate House School, Derby

Nemesis

'Mum, we've been here for over a week now and I haven't seen anything exciting,' moaned Chris.

'Well maybe something exciting will happen. If you stop moaning,' replied Mum.

Chris sighed and went to his room.

When Chris was in his room, he started to hear banging noises coming from the attic.

'What's that?' mumbled Chris to himself. 'I'm going to go and see.'

So Chris slowly went up the stairs and as he got nearer, the sound got louder. When he reached the top, he opened the door and quickly ran to turn on the light.

The first thing he saw was a wooden chest. Chris went closer to the chest and opened it. Inside were some pictures, notes and letters. There were also some jewels. The first thing he noticed was his own name on one of the envelopes. Puzzled and strangely frightened, Chris quickly tore the envelope open and read it. It was dated 14th June 1893.

As he read it, he felt the hairs rising on the back of his neck.

'Dear Chris Brown

When you read this, it will be September 7th 2005 and the time will be 7.15am. You are never going to escape from the attic, the lights are going to turn off and the door is going to slam shut.

I look forward to meeting you soon.

5 ... 4 ... 3 ... 2 ... 1'.

Then all of a sudden Chris dropped the letter in fear. As he did so, the door slammed and the light went off ...

Sanita Chopra (12)
Friargate House School, Derby

Siege On Bruma

Intro

Uriel Semtpim, Emperor of Tamriel. The Daedric Oblivion Gates linking Tamriel to the planes of Oblivion. A heroine locked in a cell awaiting death.

The Story

Rei the mistaken convict awaits execution. 'The Oblivion Crisis has begun,' says the prisoner across the corridor looking across through the window. Rei the heroine soon climbs up the wall to the window, she peers out to see this so called 'Oblivion Crisis'. Orange flames lick her cheeks and she is forced back by the heat. When she hits the ground she loses consciousness. She awakes in a tavern surrounded by drunken patrons slurping brandy and then some guards burst through the door, then hit her over the head with something blunt and drag her away.

When she awakes for the second time, she is sitting in a chair wearing shining gold and black armour with an enchanted sword lying in a gold and black scabbard glowing like a mythical sun. The chair is twenty-four carat gold with quilted red velvet cushions, in front of her is a young man staring at her, like a beggar opposite a three-course dinner. Then he speaks, 'Welcome to the Imperial Palace. I am Uriel Semtpim, Emperor of Tamriel and you have been chosen by me to help end the 'Oblivion Crisis'. Do you accept?'

Rei opens her mouth but as she is about to speak a messenger bursts into the room and whisks her away. They leave the building and stand on the balcony, the weather is non-existent. The sky is just red like running blood, the trees around the castle are burning and in the middle of this commotion is a giant orange flame melting away. When the flame has melted it left a black stone archway with a bubble of fire inside. Then suddenly millions of Daedra come flooding out burning everything as they try to storm the castle. It was then that we retreat back to the room. Then the Emperor draws a deep breath and asks, 'What is your name heroine?'

Rei is amazed to hear 'Heroine', then she tells him, 'My name is Rei.' He asks her if she knew what that flame was. She answers, 'No,' but tells him that she has seen it before in the prison. 'I climbed up the wall to look out of the window and I got burnt by one of those gates I fell and woke up in the tavern' ...

Thomas Long (14)
Furrowfeld School, Gateshead

The Warriors

Revenge is so sweet!

The wolf a tough, hard, nasty gang leader who ruled by fear, was holding one of his most important meetings.

Panther and Cheetah, second in command, were outside training the other gang members. It was a cold, dark night, the wind whipping up the tension in the group. The atmosphere was violent but electric as everyone was pumped up for the big fight which was taking place later that night.

Wolf gathered his cubs together for a big talk. They needed to discuss tactics as they were heavily outnumbered. They were going to strike hard, no one was going to firebomb their territory and get away with it. Wolf could still see the hellish fire destroying his den. He could hear the screams from his family cutting through his whole body.

He gathered his cubs. Tonight was the night, fireworks were about to explode, the fight was on! They had a good idea where they thought they were. As they approached they saw a shadow in the mist. They got closer to the shadow and noticed an even larger shadow just behind. They had found the Baseball Furries. They stood with their baseball bats, there was an eerie silence and then all of a sudden all hell let loose. The silence was broken with battle cries and the clattering of bats lashing out in the mist. It seemed like hours but it must have only lasted minutes, we were victorious the Furries had fallen.

George Morris (14)
Furrowfeld School, Gateshead

Rome

I craved one day to fight in the coliseum like my father. He was great, until Maximus a 15-year-old that had talent for killing and would go down as one of the greats in history. As he fought with his sword, his stance was amazing. The way he slashed his opponent was like watching a swift wind knock down thousands of men. My father would have won. The reason he didn't was because Maximus had no loyalty, he struck my father down when he wasn't looking. He won 137 fights in the coliseum and my father won 83 until he was killed.

My name is Alexander Croft, I have won 18 fights but not in the coliseum. In 5 days time I've my first fight there against Drake Rogers, a young fighter who had only won 7 fights.

I made an impressive start lashing out at him with my sword, his shield blocking everything. Suddenly he hit me, his shield dropped. I punched him, then threw my sword at him. It was over. I went on to win 69 more fights in the coliseum. My fight with Maximus lasted 48 minutes. He caught my shoulder with a knife and knocked me down. He thought he had won, as he waved to the crowd, I got up and stabbed him. I had my revenge!

Story by Jack Lee.

'Carl have you found something in the ruins of the coliseum?'
   'Yes, it's a story it's at least 300 years old!'

Christopher Morrison (13)
Furrowfeld School, Gateshead

Street Racing

He walked into his bedroom and sat down in the floor seat. The floor seat looked like a rally car driver's seat, but the frame wasn't there - just padding - like a seat with a steering wheel attached to it and pedals. He switched a silver button and the light went from red to green. A hand reached out and picked up the remote control from the floor and the television sprang to life.

Loading ...

Midnight Club 3

The boy kept his finger on X and the map appeared and he found a race. He pushed his right foot down and the Nissan Skyline shot forward. The road ahead was lit by the beams from the car's headlights and frequent street lights. The engine roared as he pressed down further on the accelerator. The boy pressed down on R1 and the car zigzagged and suddenly flipped. For a brief moment the screen flickered then a blinding light sprang from the television. There was a piercing scream and then silence. All he saw was a blank screen then footsteps thudded up the staircase and a woman burst into the bedroom, nothing.

An empty car seat; the television screen flickered and a blurred image came into focus. What looked like it could have been a Nissan Skyline was crushed against a dark wall. A body was half in it.

Liam Dodds (13)
Furrowfeld School, Gateshead

Diving Competition

'And the next contestant is Debbie Sands from Lancashire!'

Debbie emerged from the changing rooms to a crowd of cheering school children. Her face was smiling, her hands were waving but her heart was screaming. 'Get out, go back and get out!'

Debbie stepped up to the ladder as the noise from the crowd died away. She looked over at her parents who had anxious smiles on their faces then back at the ladder. Her heart was still shouting at her but she couldn't turn back now. She took a deep breath and put one foot on the first rung of the ladder. No going back now. She began to climb the twenty feet. Step by step.

When she reached the top, there was no sound from anyone, only her heart, now screaming at her at full blast. The sodden rubber squelched under her feet from the other people who had used it that day. She slowly walked to the edge, had one last look at the crowd, took her position and jumped. She twirled, twisted, pirouetted and swirled until she hit the water with a gigantic splash.

Debbie's head emerged triumphantly from the water to meet rounds of applause and cheering. She swam over to the steps and was helped out by her classmates, all of them patting her on the back and congratulating her. The crowd fell silent again but soon continued to cheer as the announcer declared that Debbie Sands had won the competition.

Sarah Taylor (12)
Honley High School, Holmfirth

A Wolf Story

If only I hadn't done it, Father had warned me against it, there were wolves in the woods. I mean, everyone knew that. I had known it since I was a kid. How could I have been so stupid?

I had wandered into the forest. OK, so I had stormed once again into the forest after yet another violent argument with my dad. I had always gone into the woods by our village, but this time, the argument had been bigger than normal, and I had wandered further than normal into the woods. It was then that I came upon a lone cub, without a she-wolf in sight. I went looking for the she-wolf and her mate, and then I saw it, a bronze-coloured she-wolf and a grey, fierce-looking male, covered with blood, lying in the dirt.

I began to feel sorry for the wolf, its mother gone, just like mine, and no father either. So I picked up the wolf cub that was walking towards me, and took it home.

I knew Dad wouldn't let me keep him, and so I hid him from sight. I put him in my small bedroom in the cabin, (Dad never comes in there, probably because it's a bit of a mess.) And soon, without knowing it, a connection formed that would soon make us not just a wolf and human, but much more!

Jacob Quesne (12)
Honley High School, Holmfirth

In The Morning

Unzipping the triangular black make-up bag, I smiled happily. Rummaging around, I found what I was looking for. A silver rectangular tin, with a sliding lid. *Perfect,* I thought. Dipping my finger into the tub, I smoothly applied the thick, red substance to my unsightly lips. My new lipgloss suited me perfectly!

Next, I pulled out a glass bottle and squirted the fragrance on my wrists. It ran down my arm and I quickly rubbed it in. My penultimate item was a pen-shaped, doublesided mascara bush. I brushed it onto my eyelashes which instantly elongated them. I fluttered my eyes and admired my work.

Finally, I found my mini blue Vaseline tub and put it in my black trouser pocket. I zipped up the make-up bag and put it back in my wardrobe. Rushing hurriedly downstairs, whilst putting my hair in a loose ponytail, I munched on a slice of toast. Gasping, I ran back upstairs, realising I had forgotten my socks …

Gulping down a glass of fruit juice, I put on my waterproof and fetched my bag. Then, slipping on my scuffed shoes, I unlocked the door and said bye to my mum and dad. Stepping outside, I zipped up my coat and pulled up the hood. I met my neighbour, halfway down the road and set off to the bus stop. After dodging puddles, I arrived in the village and said hi to my friends. Moments later, and the bus came. Flashing my bus pass, I clambered on and sat down. Phew! Over for another day …

Lauren Cocking (11)
Honley High School, Holmfirth

The Battle Of Parnium 9

Thud, thud, thud, our auto rifles blasted at the Arachnids who were tearing apart our soldiers.

Our tanks blasted a bridge to buy us more time from infected base 14. Our unit had abandoned 4 main control centres and 16 small bunkers from the main line. But this time we were going to defend the river at all costs. We blew apart all the small walkways across the river and dug in ready to fight for the gods. Our artillery fired away and took large chunks out of their army but the gaps just filled in with more of them. Then our worst nightmare happened ... Hundreds of flying bugs with talons and claws those were larger than the tallest man in our unit.

'Battle stations!' the captain yelled.

'Argh!' a young trooper cried.

'Argh! Shuuur.' A trooper gargled in his own blood.

Then a big machine-gun half track pulled up and a rather exhausted driver fell out with huge flesh wounds to the chest and arms.

'Hey you trooper!' Was the captain shouting at me? Then I pointed to myself and he yelled, 'Yes! You get on that gun!'

So I did and wow it was powerful, loads dropping down like flies to the awesome gun.

'We need evac now Sir,' then out of nowhere Pegasus jet fighters came in and unlashed the gods' fury on the bugs.

'They're retreating,' someone yelled.

'Yeah! Yeah! Yeah haaa!' we all cheered.

We got our stuff and marched. I managed to catch a ride on a MKIII destroyer tank. The ride was easy, just scouts we took out.

Then, out of nowhere bugs charged; this time they weren't the flyers. These were the giant 15ft tall claws and teeth arachnids, throwing all of us about.

'Argh!' I yelled. I must have killed roughly 20 before a screaming pain hit me in my stomach.

Aidan Flanagan (12)
Honley High School, Holmfirth

The Pet Palace

We're driving in the car and my little sister Jessica kept on saying, 'Are we there yet?'

My dad kept on saying over and over again, '*No!*'

Until about half an hour after we'd set off, then Mum said, 'We're here.'

Me and Jessica jumped out the car and rushed into the Pet Palace, we looked at every pet including dogs, cats, birds, fish and even turtles, but nothing made us want to buy anything, but then I spotted a sign that read: *Baby Animals* so me and my sister rushed to it and saw the cutest cat ever, it was a browny-grey with black stripes and a little black nose.

We bought her and took her home. We named her Tiny because she was so small but my sister wanted to call her Tiffany, we stuck on Tiny. We played 'parties', Jessica and me had party hats on, but we felt like we left Tiny out so we made her a tiny hat but she just scratched it up. Every year on Tiny's birthday we'd make her a hat and give her a small present, which was normally a tiny piece of cat food.

After nine years Tiny passed away, we were all upset because we had such a great time with Tiny.

Jemma Martin (12)
Honley High School, Holmfirth

My Hero

… 'And Spiderman saved the day again!'

Yawn yawn. My brother watches the most distasteful programmes on the planet! I mean what kind of weirdo would actually believe in all that 'Flying men in leotards' stuff anyway? Well not me. I hate it so much! It drives me bonkers, crazy, bats, whatever. 'Mu-um, I'm going upstairs to do my homework,' I yell at the kitchen door.

Sure, I'm really gonna do my homework? More like phone up Sal and see what Bex and Crissy are up to!

'OK Babe, but before you do can you nip out and fetch us a sarnie?' my mum asks.

She can easily get up and fetch herself one! But seeing as I'm a little angel, I get up and go to get her one. So here I am outside ready to … what is that? Is it some kind of aeroplane? No, it's too small even to be a glider. Oh, well I suppose I'll just … I hear the squeak of brakes. I turn to look at the car coming towards me. Time stands still, I get ready to feel the road's gravel on my face when I feel someone's arms around me. 'Who are you?' I ask, not daring to look, it could be a madman!

'I am Superman!'

I turn round. It's a man in a leotard! And I'm flying! In a poof of smoke he is gone! I am at my front door.

'Where's my sandwich?' asks Mum.

'Well … let's just say, Superman ate it?' Well it's not every day you get saved by a guy in a leotard, is it?

Alice Peach (12)
Lees Brook Community Sports College, Derby

Miss Scary Mary

'Only ten years old and she's gone, what a terrible mother I am!'

'Don't take it out on yourself dear.'

In 1991 on Foxglove Street, lay a 10-year-old in the cemetery, whose name was Mary. Mary was a good, quiet little girl. She'd never hurt anyone or anything; she's her mother's sunshine, although she got bullied. Ten days later her mother found a letter on an unusual day. As her mother came towards the letter, in shock, she pierced the envelope and pulled out a letter. She was shaking like a cold fish, the mother read it, with a horrified face as it said: 'I'll get them, I'll get them!' Her mother stopped dead. All of a sudden Mary's father walked in the room and realised that Emily, Mary's mother, was standing shocked in the same spot holding a piece of paper. The writing was the colour red, like a big splash of blood.

'Who's that from?'

'Mary!'

'Don't be stupid, it can't be Ma -'

'Yes it is!'

Bang! went the letter on a table.

'I want to see the police.'

'What! Why?'

'I love my daughter and she loves me. I won't let her down. That's final!' Emily walked out of the door with a slam and left her husband to call the police. *Bang!* went the phone as Fred, Mary's father, was angry. He had to do something to the letter and quick.

Five minutes later Emily came back from her ten minute walk and found a letter ripped up. Was it Fred who'd killed Mary?

Chelsea Cooper (12)
Lees Brook Community Sports College, Derby

Save The Werewolf

I heard a bang downstairs. It sounded like it was coming from the basement, so I went down to see what it was. I walked down the cold, creaky stairs, the wind blew the door shut, I felt extremely scared. I could hear wolves howling outside through the crack in the window. I heard something rustling in boxes, I saw something scatter across the room, it was cold, damp and the room looked very big. The only light I had was the moonlight coming through the window. I walked further down the stairs, they started to creak. I fell dramatically.

'I think I've sprained my ankle. Ow!' I screamed with tears running down my face. I could taste them dripping down like a tap or rain rolling down the window.

I woke up in a dark, gloomy graveyard. I could see lots of gravestones through the mist, and creatures wearing cloaks. I didn't know how I'd got there. I got up off the damp, hard floor, I sneaked passed them limping on my bad ankle. I don't think they saw me, then suddenly my heart started pumping louder. I felt it ripping out of my chest, I just saw a huge werewolf, I shivered, I felt paralysed. I wanted to move but my body wouldn't let me. He came towards me, I tried to run but he pounced on me like I was his prey, he scratched my face harder, the cuts got deeper and deeper. I didn't know what to do, I tried to get him off, but he wouldn't move, I thought I was going to die.

Jessica Clancy (12)
Lees Brook Community Sports College, Derby

Zombified

One stormy day, deep down in the graveyard, lived the Zocarac. All you could see were zombies' gravestones shaking and a gate banging. Voices screaming through the distance. The moonlight shining straight down in the graveyard. Dead souls calling; surrounding the Zocarac in the air. It feeds on humans or other monsters, no matter what, but it mostly feeds on the dead. There were dragons in the far distance.

Its razor blade on its head stronger than steel. The claws like a million slashes striking. The fangs, sharp as everything you could imagine; it's easily deadly. It was a place darker than you had ever seen.

Suddenly a human approached; they chopped him aggressively with their razor blades. The human screamed; he suddenly died. Then they ate him from their hunger. The moonlight grew into a dark red, gazing within its anger. Dark blue liquid ran down from the moon, attacking the Zocarac. They were inflammable, from the evil dark blue liquid. The moon turned dark black. The Zocarac had to escape. All the graveyards were full of dark liquid.

There was a spell caster named Thornazon who caused all the graveyards to flow with the liquid. He stood deep down in the green gloomy mist. Bats screeching, guarding the throne. Venom squirting quickly like a spirited fountain, black thunder and lightning struck throughout the mist. Stones flew within the comaya winds. The zombies grew stronger. I gave them powers from every wind that attached to them. He was the strongest magician. The war began …

Michael Aston (12)
Lees Brook Community Sports College, Derby

Disaster On Flight 717

The plane shuddered as it slowly taxied down the runway. Matt sat in his seat on Flight 717 to Melbourne, Australia. He was leaving London to go to his mum's funeral. Matt had dark blue eyes and fair blond hair and wore worn jeans and a dirty T-shirt. He hadn't slept in days and his face showed it. The plane shook as the engines prepared to accelerate the plane down the runway. Then without warning the plane went flying forward and after what seemed like an eternity lifted off the ground.

His ears stung as the air pressure changed inside the cabin and then after five minutes the plane levelled out and the seatbelt sign went off. A waitress was coming round but he decided to grab a pillow and, after what felt like hours, drifted into a restless sleep.

There was a deafening screech and he woke to find his head was bleeding and oxygen masks had been released. The plane plummeted downwards heading straight for the ocean. There was screaming and a baby crying. Everyone knew they were going to die. Then there was a smash and everything went black.

Matt woke up in agonising pain on some sort of rock. His vision was blurry and his legs were in agony. He managed to look round to see that others weren't so lucky. The sea was littered with dead bodies like the aftermath of a battle. It was a horrific sight. The few badly wounded survivors struggled to make it onto the rock.

There was no chance for survival. Matt knew he was going to die.

Nicholas Adams (12)
St Michael's Catholic High School, Watford

A Day In The Life Of Ashley Young

I first wake up and I smell a lovely breakfast which contains sausage, bacon, black and white pudding, burgers and bread with some tomato ketchup. Then I go and work out in my gym. I have everything. I need to keep fit and healthy. When I'm ready to go I have a quick jog around the park.

Then I travel up town in my new Mazda MX5. When I arrive at Vicarage Road, I train with the team like Marlon King, Jay Demerit, Darius Henderson and Gavin Mahan.

Then there is a meeting about the play offs against Crystal Palace. That's what Aidy Boothroyd was talking about. We go and train again for an hour and then we all head home.

The next day it was the big day, when we first go out on the pitch the atmosphere was incredible. There were millions of fans singing and cheering. The whistle had gone and it started. We had so many chances but the keeper kept on saving them all. The whistle was blown, it was half-time. The second half had started, we had taken the lead thanks to Marlon. Then after a while I scored a free kick, we were winning 2-0. Later on Mathew Spring scored, soon after it was full-time. We had won 3-0. Aidy Boothroyd congratulated us.

Louise Leahy (11)
St Michael's Catholic High School, Watford

The Baker

Once upon a time there was a village called Heaven Hempstead. It was filled with lots of merry people except for one man, known as the evil gingerbread baker. He lived on a hill on the outskirts of the village. The gingerbread baker was working on a monster, he had been working on this monster for as long as I could remember, so nobody was ever expecting it to be finished anytime soon. He had always said it was invisible and it would kill everyone, the man was mad so I didn't worry.

The next day was Heaven Day, everyone was happy and having fun, when suddenly an epic monster smashed through the village. It smashed every building and killed every man and woman it set eyes on. The devil had gingerbread pistols and even though it was said to be invincible, it had one tiny weakness … it was edible.

It wasn't long until the mayor found out about the devil, and he wasn't very merry then. The mayor had an idea to build a robot to eat the devil.

So the next day the robot was built and sent out into the big wide world. The village looked more like Hell Hempstead than Heaven.

When the gingerbread devil finally bumped into the robot he was lying half-eaten on the floor with a trail of crumbs beside him and a gang of hungry, merry people eating him. And they all lived happily ever after, except for the baker of course.

Corey Clarke (12)
St Michael's Catholic High School, Watford

Ghost Story

I knew this day would come, just knew it!

It was then I was lying on my bed. I heard the sound of wolves howling like the wind rushing through the trees on a cold and blustery day.

My cousin Davey told me to meet him in the Bilden Woods at 1. 30am. I did tell him I wasn't at all scared, but deep inside I was! My alarm rang loudly at 1.30am so I got dressed all in black to camouflage myself in the dark. I opened the door trying to make not one sound and set off heading towards the woody entrance.

On my way I saw lots of bats flying like gliders gliding high with the wind pushing them, that's when I got all shivery.

I could see the outline of Davey's body, whilst the mist had covered most of him up.

He was talking out loud in a strange language which I couldn't understand.

There he saw me walking up towards him. 'There you are, I thought you were too scared to come!' he said to me!

'No I'm not that much of a coward!' I hissed back. He ran off leaving me tagging on behind. I tried to follow but couldn't keep up. 'I knew he would do this, that was his evil plan, just run off to try and scare me, well it didn't work,' I whispered, hoping he could hear me, but again deep inside I was horrified.

So I finally found my way out *alive!* I got back into bed and set off to sleep.

I woke up the next morning and heard someone weeping quietly. I went downstairs and saw Mum crying watching the news. 'Mum what's wrong?'

'Oh you haven't heard yet?' said Mum, sadly.

'No, what is it Mum?'

'It's your cousin, my nephew Davey, he died last night, police found his body hidden under a bush in the Bilden Woods, no one knows how he got there!'

I collapsed to the floor thinking, *it could have been me!*

Rosie Moneypenny (13)
St Michael's Catholic High School, Watford

Angel In The Sky

My mum was 24 weeks pregnant when her waters broke suddenly. She lived in Ireland, her home town, and that is where she met my dad. The day she went into premature labour was just like any other. She was at my nan and grandad's house when suddenly her nightmare began. As soon as she realised what was going on she called my dad for help. She got rushed to hospital where doctors tried to stop the baby from being born. But there was no time, the baby had to be born, 16 weeks early.

My mum had a natural birth and the delivery didn't last long, as the baby was so small. She was born during the daytime. My mam had given birth to a tiny baby girl weighing half the weight of a bag of sugar and at the length of 10 inches long. My mum and dad were weak and frantic with worry, and my mum was wracked with guilt and blaming herself.

They named her Nova Mary Flannery. She was born on the 18th August 1992. Nova means 'angel in the sky'. She was placed in a tiny incubator attached to dozens of wires, keeping her alive.

As she got through the first day, my parents thought there might be a chance she could survive and live. As she got through a day and a half and seemed to be doing OK, my mum was able to pick her up for the first time without disturbing any of her life support machine. My mum picked her up and she seemed to be OK. She supported her tiny head when she felt a wet patch on her head, in horror she realised it was blood, she was bleeding from a tiny hole in her head. During all that commotion and alarm going off, she opened her beautiful blue eyes for a split second and then shut them. She passed away peacefully in my mum's arms. My mum and dad were numb with grief. Her funeral was on my dad's birthday, her tiny white coffin was carried and she was buried near my great nan in Ireland.

Denise Flannery (12)
St Michael's Catholic High School, Watford

Whispers In The Dark

'Jessica.' I was there in the cold of night listening to what I thought was my name being whispered. 'Jessica.' There it was again. Was it my mind playing tricks on me or was it really happening? That's when I woke up. I always wake up there. You see I've had this dream for a fortnight. In the dreams I'm in the dark with nothing around me but trees and every couple of minutes my name is being whispered. I don't know what it could mean!

'Jessica you're going to be late for school.'

School this school that, that's all my family cares about. But I take a different approach to school. I want to do well and have a good future and everything but it doesn't mean I have to like it, but *no* that isn't good enough for them.

'Jessica the bus is outside.'

'Run!'

After school I usually go for a run in the woods, but today I went home, got changed and had a packet of crisps. I watched some TV, nothing good was on. It was five o'clock and my mum didn't get in till six. I could go for a run in the woods even if it was getting dark, so I did just that.

I was lost. It was pitch-black I could just make out the trees … this reminded me a lot of my dream.

'Jessica.'

No it couldn't be. It must be my mind playing tricks on me. I ran a bit faster.

'Jessica.'

There it was again.

'Jessica.'

I looked behind me and saw … a *ghost!*

'Jessica die.'

And I did just that.

Shannon Flaherty (12)
St Michael's Catholic High School, Watford

The Watford Playoff Semi-Final

I couldn't believe my eyes. I was going to Vicarage Road Stadium. You could hear people cheering for Watford from miles back! The precinct was full of people in yellow, thousands of them. I bought my usual programme at the stall and walked past the sizzling burger vans. We got to the turnstiles and there were queues of Watford supporters. Me and my mum were sitting in the Vicarage Road End because Palace had to sit in the 'Lower Rous' where our season tickets were. I held my ticket tightly thinking it was going to get stolen.

We finally got to the front of the queue. I handed over my ticket and went into the stadium. My mum bought three Harry's 50:50 tickets as normal and went to find our seats. As I walked out into the stadium itself, I saw the bright green grass and yellow, red and black balloons, flying around in the air. Opposite the Vicarage Road End, is The Rookery and that was jam-packed with people in yellow shirts. Harry the hornet was running round the pitch dancing and waving at people.

Suddenly the person with the microphone said that the two minute bell had just gone. This made all the fans even more excited. They were singing anything they thought, for example 'Yellow Army'. This was the second leg and we had beaten them 3-0 in the first leg, so we had a headstart!

Both teams were ready so the game kicked off!

Gina Wigg (11)
St Michael's Catholic High School, Watford

A Day In The Life Of Marlon King

Sunday 21st May 2006

The coach journey was horrid, it took ages. The lads were rowdy, I could hardly hear myself think let alone sleep. On top of this the traffic was horrendous, roadworks everywhere. Eventually we arrived at the junction to exit from the motorway. Cheers were heard all over the coach, excitement was showing on the faces of the players.

After about ten minutes we saw the magnificent sight of the Millennium Stadium, the coach pulled up into the parking space which was reserved for us. The doors opened, everyone rushed towards the front of the coach urgent to get out to put all their bags in the changing rooms.

Aidy Boothroyd gave us the team talk. He said, 'Good luck with the game, keep your heads lads.' The players listened to the National Anthem, the stadium was electric singing and chanting.

Whistle blew, game commenced. Watford took the upper hand, their passing and skill on the ball was magic. The ball dropped to my feet just outside the area. I took on the first defender, went round him straight into the box, when the goalie tackled me bringing me down. The ref blew for a penalty. I got up and walked towards the penalty area knowing what had to be done. The whistle blew again, I ran towards the ball, and struck it. Goal - top left hand corner. The fans burst into cheers of 'Marlon, Marlon, Marlon King!'

The final whistle blew, we'd won the game.

Connor Welch (11)
St Michael's Catholic High School, Watford

Curiosity Killed The Cat

The Italian Trekker hacked his way through the dense Amazonian undergrowth, machete in hand, his long curly hair greasy with sweat. He swatted at the cloud of mosquitoes hovering around his head, he hated the things, and they made his life a misery.

He came to a clearing, and paused to drink from his hipflask, the cool water refreshed him after the parching hike through the forest, being followed relentlessly by the scorching Peruvian sun.

All of a sudden, something shiny caught the Italian's eye, he looked up to see the wreck of a crashed tour-plane embedded in the vine-infested branches above.

Minutes later he was at the top of the tree, standing in the doorway of the skeletal plane, curiosity called, and he stepped into the wreck. The plane was completely derelict, vines snaked their way through its interior, entering through the holes puncturing the plane's sides. He jumped as a rustling movement caught the corner of his eye, startling him. He turned around viciously, bearing his machete, to realise it was nothing but a tree frog that had awoken him from his stupor. He gazed around, and noticed a large overhead compartment, and decided to take a look inside, he opened it, and his stomach writhed as the carcass of a dead passenger fell limply to the floor beside him, its rotting flesh hanging from its bones, he turned in disgust and was about to run for the door, when a vice-like grip seized his ankle.

Sam O'Shea (13)
St Michael's Catholic High School, Watford

Bastet

October 3rd

These mortals think me a gentle soul. Women pray for me to give mercy and to tell my father (the sun god Ra) to stop the waters flowing with the blazing sun. But sacred tombs have been opened and offerings stolen.

At first the people thought they had outwitted me, they danced and feasted on the treasures they had taken. I will crush them into the earth until they are nothing but dust. The priests and priestesses flee to the underground safety of the tombs, what they do not know is the tombs are not safe, people lose their way in the darkness, take but one wrong turn in the labyrinth of passages and you are lost forever, few make it out of the tombs alive.

I felt the air move behind me.

'Hello Anubis,' I said as I turned to look at the one the mortals call 'Jackal'. 'Come out of the shadows my devious friend, and tell me what the god of the dead is doing in the world of the living.'

'We need to talk to Bastet, all this killing. It needs to stop, soon there will be no one left in Memphis.'

I lit a candle and the room became instantly filled with an eerie orange glow, the Jackal's eyes grew wide as he saw the damage the mortals had caused to my temple, sacred jars and statues scattered the bloodstained floor.

'Oh,' whispered the Jackal, 'I see.'

Nicole Rixon (13)
St Michael's Catholic High School, Watford

Waiting

She walked down the alleyway looking behind her broad shoulders after every step. She took a deep breath and carried on walking. It was dark, but the fluorescent glow of the street lamps lit up the dark midnight sky.

She looked around. Not many people were out this late, but even so there were a few drunken people hiding away in the darkness. She looked behind her shoulder, nothing. But as her head turned back towards the alleyway, a shadow flickered below a light.

She gasped and stumbled backwards. She dropped her rucksack and started to run back down to the park. Then she stopped. She thought about how he would still be at the park. Waiting for her. Waiting for her to give in and return to him.

She decided to walk back down the alleyway towards her house. It was the safe option. She ran to her house. Then stopped as she came up to the driveway. The light was on. She had turned it off before she had left.

She stopped to get her keys out of her bag. Then she remembered she had dropped her bag. She would have to go back to get it. She turned back. Her feet crunching on the small pebbles below her school shoes.

She walked down the alleyway, everything looked different. Then she saw it. Her rucksack was lying on the floor. She picked it up and felt around for her keys. They weren't there! She stood up. Turned around and saw a flickering shadow below a street lamp. She turned back.

He was there ... waiting.

Paloma Watson (12)
St Michael's Catholic High School, Watford

In The Life Of Angel Ross

Journal Log 75 27th September 3169

It is World War 19 we have already suffered grave losses against the robot army. Their leader, Alex Crawler, a child who invents things. He was trying to create a microchip that could put an end to violent behaviour. But it went wrong when he tested the first prototype on himself. He hadn't figured out all the kinks.

It all went terribly wrong when some of the bullies at school started picking on him so he lashed out and instead of the chip stopping him it shocked him. His brain changed, he started talking about inventing robots but no one listened to him. He started making small robots to start off with, but the chip was changing him, it was making his brain grow and the more his brain grew the more the robots grew. By the age of 14, he was making robots the size of humans. When he was 16 he had an army. No one knew how long it would be before he activated them.

This war has been going on for nearly two years now, we can't hold out much longer, we have at least 600 men. He has 6,000. I know they are coming, I can hear them. If they breach the main hall I know I'm dead.

Oh no they have breached the main hall, I hope someone gets this, so people can know the truth.

Joshua Melsome (12)
St Michael's Catholic High School, Watford

The Ghost Story Of The Haunted Trench

Hi, my name is Mel, short for Melany.

I live in North Yorkshire in the countryside. I live in an old trench, but obviously a home. My mum had just walked out the front door to go and feed the chickens.

She normally went to the pub after she'd fed the chickens, so I was all alone in my house, so I decided to watch TV. I turned it on, thankfully CBBC was on, great, it's Tracy Beaker.

About ten minutes went on and I started to hear some creepy noises coming from upstairs. It started getting louder and louder, I started to freak out a lot. So I crept upstairs to find, to my surprise, a horrid white mist in the air. It started turning into something. I could start to see a soldier of some sort, it came closer and closer towards me, I panicked and ran away.

Two hours went by, me sitting in the barn with my phone and laptop, waiting patiently for my mum.

The phone rang. Mum rang, she asked me if I was OK. I replied, telling her the scary story.

She wasn't very worried seeing as she was slightly drunk, she said to me, 'Stop moaning, and watch TV.' Then rudely she put the phone down on me. I was so angry!

I decided to Google the image, and to my surprise it said it was an old captain from the First World War!

I wasn't going to panic, so I decided to go over to Amy's house. I went out of the back gate and made my way down to Whippendale Park, she lived one door away.

I went to number one, Whippendale Park, I knocked. 'Hi, Mrs Kate, is Amy there?'

'Yes, Amy, Mel is here for you.'

So as I walked in I felt safe, as I was away from that freakish house!

Lily Hattingh (12)
St Michael's Catholic High School, Watford

Walls Have Ears, Windows Have Sight ...

She was a metal superstar at the Grammys. She was wining and dining with all the big stars like Twiggy Ramirez (the hottest guy ever! Oh, and his guitar playing is pretty good too) and My Chemical Romance.

'Helena, Helena!'

'Yes, Sir?'

She often daydreamed in maths.

'Would you please pay attention.'

She hated snapping back to reality. With a sigh Helena Byrne started to write; 'The many uses of algebra'. No wonder she daydreamed a lot.

Mr Colon started to drone on again, so she looked out of the window. She didn't remember how, but a gasp had escaped from her mouth.

'Helena Byrne! That's the second time you've interrupted my lesson. There had better be a good reason for this.'

'There was someone in that little garden, Sir, right outside the window!'

'What? Oh, rubbish!'

'Sir, I swear, someone was there, looking at me.'

'*Detention!* At lunchtime for ten minutes!'

The boy that sat next to her, Peter Dudey, turned to look at her, 'Lena, are you crazy! There are no doors to out there!'

'I know. That's what scares me.'

All through the lesson she barely took her eyes off that window.

What she had seen was one of the scariest things she had ever witnessed. There had been a man. A man laughing like a maniac, with what must have been all the blood in his body, running down his face.

Sherilyn Harding (12)
St Michael's Catholic High School, Watford

The New Head Of Year

'Yes! School's out!' shouted Ellen as she burst open the school doors. She was looking forward to the weekend but she was also looking forward to having a good nose at the new neighbours.

The next morning, Ellen was woken up by the sound of the removal lorry parking in next-door's driveway. Ellen peeked through her curtains inquisitively. They all looked brainy and they sounded posh as she overheard her mum, dad and Jack out on the drive greeting them. Ellen just tucked herself back into bed, after all it was Saturday.

Although Ellen had just seen them, her first impression wasn't brilliant.

The next day Ellen yanked her brother into her bedroom. 'Listen to me, we are going to have a bit of fun with our new neighbours.' Now Jack and Ellen spent the next couple of hours trying to figure out the perfect trick.

'I've got it!' screamed Ellen. 'We will swap doorbells so when all your mates come ringing the doorbell this afternoon, asking for you to come out to play football, their doorbell will be ringing like a church bell on a Sunday morning.'

Jack agreed and quickly ran to swap the doorbells. That evening Ellen overheard Charles and his wife discussing the doorbell mystery.

The weekend was over and it was time to return to school. When Ellen arrived in the hall for assembly, her headmaster Mr Beverly was waiting for them.

'Good morning children, I would like to introduce your new head of year Mr Charles Elsberry.'

Mr Beverly had just dropped a gigantic bombshell in Ellen's world.

Emily Butcher (11)
St Michael's Catholic High School, Watford

Graveyard Ghouls

Wandering through graveyards late at night isn't most people's idea of fun, but then Georgia wasn't most people. As an avid reader of horror stories she had a plan to write her own, and tonight was research. Babbling excitedly into her dictaphone, things were going tremendously.

As Georgia perched on the granite gravestone she felt a strange sensation; a feeling that she was being watched. She turned around, exploring the surroundings for anything peculiar or abnormal. Suddenly a chill ran down her spine and Georgia felt the colour drain from her chubby, little face.

Standing on the gravel path in front of her was a vague, shadowy figure. Georgia couldn't make out any features ... until a freak flash of lightning lit up the sky, unluckily Georgia saw a bit more than she wanted to! The mysterious figure was dressed in black, a glossy top hat and black cloak. As it stood, his cape wafted in the midnight breeze.

Georgia dashed towards the churchyard gates. She ran and ran, staggering as she zigzagged through the headstones. Despite the race, the creepy figure caught up. His grey, lifeless hand clasped her fleece. He spun her round. Georgia's eyes were transfixed on the vampire's face. Georgia stared at the intimidating vampire, his teeth bloodstained and pointed.

Whilst Georgia stood hypnotised, he sank his fangs into her neck. At the break of dawn Georgia's motionless body lay on the pathway. Georgia's corpse lay unaccompanied with only a trickle of crimson blood on her neck.

Adele Rayner (12)
St Michael's Catholic High School, Watford

The Wedding

It was a very refreshing morning, and Susie felt the wind whistle through her hair.

Susie was feeling her very last blast of freedom, as today was her wedding day.

2nd January 2006 was the day, she was to become Mrs Smith.

The house was full of action and she longed to stay in the spring breeze for just a few more minutes more ... when Cilla, her six-year-old niece, came calling, 'Susie, Susie, there's someone on the phone.' In a hurry she ran in the house and picked up the phone. But her face quickly changed from the excited smile to a tearful child. Not wishing to discuss with anyone, she put the phone down and continued getting ready for the big wedding.

She was a plain girl and really didn't like too much pampering, so getting ready was simple.

The girls helping her left one by one and she was left thinking if she was doing the right thing. *Should I marry him or should I not? Am I marrying the right person? How can I let everyone down?*

The doorbell rang and her dad was there ready to collect her and take her to the church.

The church was only two miles away from home, but it felt like it was the longest journey ever. As they were getting closer and closer, Susie felt more nervous.

Then finally when they arrived Susie started to shout, 'I can't do this!' Susie's Dad heard and tried to give her as much support as he possible could, so Susie agreed and as she was walking down the aisle, she began to cry. At the altar she was about to say 'I do' when she heard a man shout at the back of the church, 'No! Susie don't do it, don't marry him ...'

Ciara Stewart (12)
St Michael's Catholic High School, Watford

A Day In The Life Of ...

Today has to have been one of the worst days so far; I got homework from nearly every lesson! But that's not the end of it, I also found out that my so-called best friend not only likes my ex-boyfriend, *but* has been to see a movie with him!

Surely there's a rule about not betraying your friends for the sake of a boy? I pretended that I didn't care, and told her that it was fine, hoped they would be happy but inside it felt like devastating attacks were happening. We've been friends since nursery and I have decided that no matter how hard it is, I won't tell her that it hurts me. Boys come and go but friends are forever.

Mom and Dad are arguing again! They think that I'm asleep. I hope that they aren't going to get divorced! Sasha said that she hated it when her parents got divorced because she has to move between two houses and as if that wasn't bad enough, her dad's girlfriend moved in and now there's two sets of rules.

I want to do 100 sit ups a day and skip for five minutes. I feel that my clothes are too tight for me, and when I went shopping with Sasha we were trying on clothes, when I asked her if my bum looked big, she said it was huge.

Better go! Hope tomorrow is a better day.

Regan Kerr (11)
St Michael's Catholic High School, Watford

Death Mountain

Sean was on a school trip, he had just left Luton airport on Flight 715 for France, and so far everything was going fine until they were flying over the Alps and the engines began to fade. Suddenly the plane was spinning out of control and the pilot was struggling to keep it airborne, but it was too late and the plane crashed into the side of the mountain. The pilot and over half the passengers were dead, and others were horrifically injured.

The first night was the worst night in Sean's life. It was unbearably cold and there was no food. They could make water from the snow and ice, but that didn't help their hunger. There was no chance of repairing the plane, as one of the wings had broken off in the crash. Their only hope was that they would be rescued.

After a few days life on the mountain was starting to get really tough, a few more people had died from their injuries, and the few people left were beginning to starve. There was nothing to eat, except … each other. They had to eat the flesh of the dead in order to survive. It felt wrong and tasted disgusting, but cannibalism was the only way to stay alive.

So there they were reluctantly feasting on human flesh for almost three weeks. It was the worst and longest three weeks in Sean's life, but there was no choice, eat … or die. Eventually they were rescued but the cold had claimed more lives and some refused to eat and just starved to death, so in the end there was only about twenty or thirty of them left, if that, it was a small plane and there hadn't been a whole lot of people on board, but there was one thing for sure, it had been an experience none of them would forget.

Sean Beasley (13)
St Michael's Catholic High School, Watford

A Day In The Life Of Me!

The too familiar tones of my alarm clock awoke me with a start for the third day running. I stumbled out of bed to find the mess I fell asleep to still present on my floor. Half asleep, I staggered to the door and went into the hall to find my mum shouting at me for being late. This brought me back down to earth with a crash. I ran to the shower and changed, not having time for breakfast and ran out of the door. I sprinted to the bus stop to see the bus pulling away from the stop. Frustrated I waited at the bus stop for half an hour knowing that I would be late for school again.

Eventually when I got to school the bell for the first lesson had gone. I walked to the geography room, my heart sinking further with every step. Geography isn't my best subject and it's a double lesson first thing on Wednesday morning.

He approached me, the only thing I could think of was, *he's going to kill me, on my gravestone it would say 'death by geography teacher'.* As you can probably tell I don't like geography, well actually I don't like a lot of my subjects.

As the day moved on it came to lunchtime, yet again I'm doing my homework that I should have done four days ago. I was dreading my next lesson, I had one more to sit through and that was the dreaded English, hopefully I will be able to enter this competition and win.

Abbie Slade (12)
St Michael's Catholic High School, Watford

Loud Enough To Kill Someone!

There once lived an old woman who lived in a four-storey flat on the second floor. She lived on her own apart from her five cats. She lived a happy life until one day.

The woman had lived in the flat most of her life. One day a young couple moved in just above her. They were the loudest people in the whole block of flats. They played music late into the night. The woman complained of having a weak heart and that the music made it weaker.

One day the couple had a party. The music got louder and louder as the night went on. As the music got louder, the old woman's heart got weaker. She reached for the phone but before she could dial the number, she gave in and died.

When the home nurse came round the next day, she had a bit of a surprise!

Paige Coster (12)
St Michael's Catholic High School, Watford

A Day In The Life Of Figure Skates

Three days to go till the big competition. Lucy and me are really nervous. By the way Lucy is my owner, she's a great figure skater. I hope she wins the competition, it would mean the world to her.

A couple of days ago we were down at the ice rink practising. Lucy was doing wonderfully. If only she knew that. She is always telling herself how bad she is. I overheard her coach talking to her this morning, she was saying, 'Lucy if you think you can win the competition with those turns then you must have a screw loose in your head. You're capable of a lot more, you're not pushing yourself. Now get back out there and practice!'

'Yes you're right, I'm sorry.' Then she walked off. I saw her crying in front of the mirror later that day, telling herself that maybe she should drop out of the competition. I couldn't believe what she was saying. I had to get her to stay in the competition. I just had to.

We had another practice that day; I worked my hardest to help her skate like a pro. She seems happier now; I even saw her smile. She doesn't do that often not since she entered the competition anyway. It wasn't good enough though as Chloe her trainer refused to teach her. They are sending me to a rubbish skip. Goodbye Lucy you were more than my owner, you were my best friend.

Ellen Dorrian (12)
St Michael's Catholic High School, Watford

School Football

It was the end of the year at Townsend High School and Ben MacClenny was going into Year 10, and was worried about Year 10 football trials. He knew that it was going to be hard for him but he had to try his best, but he had all summer holiday to practice.

He got homework and school stuff out of the way so that he could practice as much as possible with his mates and his dad.

He was training hard but also his archenemy Justin Connelly, was going to try and slow him down, so he had to keep his wits about him and train hard.

It was the end of his six weeks and he started to get nervous, he looked up and then saw on a noticeboard: 'Year 10 football trials on Tuesday and Thursday'. Ben was ready for his trial, tomorrow was Tuesday, he could not believe it, he was very nervous.

Ben was doing really well in the trials and Justin Connelly was ill so he could not play. Ben was having the time of his life out there, played really well and before he knew it the football trial was over.

He crossed his fingers and waited for the team sheet. 'You're in the team!' said the coach.

Ben was so happy with himself, he could not believe it. He'd made it!

Louis French (12)
St Michael's Catholic High School, Watford

Hello Princess

It was dark and cold.

I was waiting for my friends at the bus stop. There was a man waiting there as well. He was tall, dark, wearing a hoodie and jeans. He didn't look nice. He kept staring at me every now and then. What should I do, text my friends saying I'd meet them somewhere else? I stayed at the bus stop, I'd been standing there for 20 minutes. The man was still there and had moved closer to me.

The bus came but the man didn't get on it. I was thinking, *where are my friends? Half an hour, I have been waiting here. We're supposed to be going to a nightclub and getting drunk.* Anyway as I looked round the man was sitting on the bench texting on his phone. I text my friends but didn't get a reply. So I started to walk home, the man looked up and stood up.

I knew he was following me, so I took a short cut through the alley. I could hear my own breathing, my lungs started to tighten, I walked faster. The man was still behind me, when I got to the end of the alley there was another man waiting there. So I turned around but bumped into the man that was at the bus stop. He said to me, 'Hello Princess ...'

Sophie Waller (12)
St Michael's Catholic High School, Watford

A Day In The Life Of Britney Spears!

People crowding around me, I felt claustrophobic shouting my name, calling at the top of their lungs. I tried to sign as many notebooks and pads as possible, but it was hard to do the same signature over and over again. Suddenly I was pushed into the bright astonishing white limo. I sat there silently with six what looked like bodyguards. We came to a halt, I saw the door beside me open, I got a glimpse of the sign it read: *Top of the Pops Recording Studio Live*

'Oh my goodness,' I said to myself. I realised I was going to have to sing.

'Miss Spears. Welcome to Top of the Pops Recording Studio Live.'

'Thanks, glad to be here.'

'Right this way,' said a cheesy, posh but snobby sounding man.

I got to what I'd seen on TV, to be a recording studio.'

'Here are your lyrics.'

'Cue the music.'

Hang on I thought, *I know this song.* All of a sudden I felt my lips moving.

'Oops I did it again!'

Thank God for that, I thought, *it is finished.*

The car pulled up to the biggest apartment I had ever seen.

'Is this my apartment?' I asked one of the six men who looked like bodyguards.

'Sure is.'

'Thanks.'

I stepped from the car searched in my pockets for my keys lifting them. Without looking I put them in the door and stepped inside. I closed the door, would anyone ever know who I really was. I wasn't sure.

Freya Bartrand (12)
St Michael's Catholic High School, Watford

The Haunted Train Carriage

Robert and his friends Jake and James and his brother Oliver were roaming around the old train yard. All there was was rusty old wheels, broken tracks and a dilapidated signal box. They looked and messed about with the controls in the signal box. Jake and James played with the old wheels and tracks, while Robert and Oliver looked in the woods for more things to do. They were in the woods for 30 second when *crash!* Something fell out of the sky. There was an old train carriage in front of the brothers. Jake and James ran over to the carriage, and they all stared in wonder.

It was a strange carriage, on the outside it was rundown, but on the inside it looked good as new. They ran up to the door which opened automatically. They crept in and the doors slammed behind them. They explored the carriage for hours until the carriage started moving. It got faster and faster and the outside world was a blur. There was screams of laughter, not from the four boys but from something out of this world.

The windows started smashing, the laughter got louder until the carriage stopped. The carriage looked different now more modern. But whatever happened the four boys ran away never to return to the train yard again.

Adam McPhail (11)
St Michael's Catholic High School, Watford

Life As A Wall

On the 2nd of February it was my birthday. I have been a wall in Mr Murphy's office in St Michael's Catholic High School in Watford for 50 years now. I have heard many voices over those years, but today I heard a voice I'd previously heard only on television. I actually heard Tony Blair talking to Mr Murphy, unfortunately they were discussing about selling the high school and knocking it down to build flats on the land.

My life was going to be crushed!

I heard many voices after that and I wanted to cry. It felt very strange, someone was talking to me and hugging me, it was weird! I've never actually been noticed before but I felt it was like a family uniting and I was part of it. I felt so pleased but also disappointed.

The next day I could hear voices whispering. I recognised the voices of the Chairman of the Governors and the caretaker, they were talking about how they could organise an objection to the plans for the new flats.

They were talking loudly to each other saying that there won't be enough schools in the area to take all the students, we are a good school and our staff are all highly qualified and they may all lose their jobs! Why does St Michael's have to be the school that closes? It does not deserve to be knocked down, there is nothing wrong with this school and it won't be closing!

Laura Stanbrook (12)
St Michael's Catholic High School, Watford

A Day In The Life Of A Dying Child In A Poor Country

It's early in the morning and I hear screams coming from everywhere I look, with more screams coming from the central town, London, England. I still can't believe how England went from being so rich, to bankrupt in two months.

I haven't eaten since the day after England went bankrupt. If we didn't have a party we wouldn't be starving, and dying of malnutrition. But it's all the past. I've just got to try and forget it.

There were 46 deaths over one night, that's the worst number of deaths so far but it will get worse.

Everyone is trying to make it to London. I'm not sure why, but I want to find out. It may be something that helps me and my sister. My parents died over night with the rest of our relations that are less than 20 miles from us.

20 minutes later

I can see the bodies coming over the hill right now. I haven't seen my sister today and I think she's in the rest of the dead bodies.

I start to have a look for her among the dead bodies; about halfway through my glance around, a shout comes out. They said the final body count was 106 which is around double our old record. I turn my head to look at the unbearable open eye stare of some of the dead bodies, as soon as I start glaring back at the bodies I see my sister, just lying there.

She's gone too.

Kieran Kelly (12)
St Michael's Catholic High School, Watford

A Day In The Life: Norm

I stood up as I heard my owner, Haddy, awake for school. As she placed her feet towards the floor she yawned, made her bed, then she drew the curtains to open her window. I could feel the draught of fresh air which I couldn't blame her for. It was a sultry day.

She put her alarm clock off and gave it a surprised look. Therefore loped to the bathroom door and got dressed, then left. When she left I didn't have anyone to scurry to that would harass me and comfort me, so all I did was sleep and eat. Haddy's the only one that adores me. Bless.

When she came back I ran to her with ecstasy and bliss. She cried my name out with pleasure while launching her oppressive bag to the floor. My tail danced from side to side just as she sprung me towards her uniform. I was really delighted when I saw her. She put me on the floor and answered the door.

It was her sister and her new family. She had had a baby boy and called it Aidan. I perceived that I wasn't going to be the cosset of the house anymore. I began to feel envy. I'm just three months old. I should still have decency with my owner.

But they obviously didn't think so!

Haddy Gibril (12)
St Michael's Catholic High School, Watford

Hello Sunshine!

I was on my way back from my best friend's party when I decided to take a short cut through the alley. It was a cold night and I just wanted to get home.

All of a sudden I heard a muffled scream coming from the bush, it was a muffled scream at first, but then got louder and louder, this was blood-curdling, I was trembling and at that time I could hear my own breath and the slightest rustle of a bush.

I started to quicken my step but then I felt a tickle on my neck, I turned around and there was no one there, I decided to ignore it, but that mysterious tickle came again.

I was so scared, I was shaking in my boots. I didn't know what to do, and just as everything went silent, someone pulled me back, pinned me down and his hands clutched round my neck, his words were ...

'Hello sunshine!'

Georgia Mays (11)
St Michael's Catholic High School, Watford

A Day In The Life Of A Fly

A fly is an impressive insect. They never seem to get bored. They just fly in circles and eat. When you see them they always seem to be drunk, it's strange they might be, you can't know.

They start the day by buzzing around waking people up, then they search the house for someone's breakfast. They happily germ-up all the food.

Then the fly will either buzz around annoying people or find a bin to pick around in.

This is continuous all day in pattern, eat, annoy someone. But occasionally they dodge a fly swat or any weapon a human can find to kill the fly with.

As a treat some days the fly might find a big smelly lump of dog poo, they roll about and get covered in it.

Sometimes I wish I were a fly!

Katherine Vovrosh (13)
St Michael's Catholic High School, Watford

A Day In My Dog's Footsteps

I wake up and get up from my grey cushion in my black bed. I bark really loud then Bradley comes down the stairs and let's me into the back garden. I pick up my chew toy, then I go and do a poo near the trampoline, then I come in, have some water and some food.

The family all give me a stroke then everyone goes to work or school. I lay on the sofa in the playroom then at 12 Phillip comes home and has his lunch, he makes me mine and tops up my water.

At 4 Bradley, Kelly and Harry come back from school. I sit on Bradley's bed while he does his homework, then me and Harry go and play in the garden. Harry gets a ball and chucks it and I go and fetch it, that is really fun.

At dinner time I go inside and lay on the floor while the family is eating dinner. After dinner the family have a bath and they watch TV and Kelly strokes me, then it is time for bed.

Bradley Bennett (13)
St Michael's Catholic High School, Watford

SBS

Experiment SBS smashed out of the containment tank and ripped off five people's heads, it ran through the window of the London Dungeon and ran for it. We already knew where it would head for. This experiment is a silver back gorilla fused with a shark we call it SBS. As you may already know sharks can't survive without water, but silver backs can, so every 4 hours SBS has to go into water for an hour, or it will die. We created SBS to be the ultimate weapon, it went wrong, now we have to get the four members of the elite force to stop SBS.

The elite force have all the information on what happened, they knew SBS wasn't far because they had a tracker planted into SBS. The members of the elite force knew this would be a difficult mission. Ben, Ryan, Charlie and Adam set out.

They split up onto roofs, the tracker indicated SBS was high up, they knew he wouldn't be there long, he needed water in 20 minutes. They surrounded SBS from all sides, they charged for SBS. SBS picked up Charlie and Adam and threw them off the roof, they put a tranquilliser bullet into the head of SBS. SBS was dizzy. Ryan shot multiple bullets at SBS, they hit SBS, so SBS charged for Ryan and went off the building with Ryan. Only Ben was left, SBS had 30 seconds to get to water, by the time he got down it was too late.

Ben Young (12)
St Michael's Catholic High School, Watford

Ghost Story

I was in my house with a few mates watching a film, when suddenly, I heard noises from upstairs. I asked Luke and Mark if they'd heard it, they said, 'Heard what? A noise from upstairs, no.' Cups started to smash from the kitchen. I was getting worried at that point. I said to Mark and Luke, 'There's a ghost in the house.' We started screaming. The ghost grabbed Luke and brought him upstairs. Me and Mark were calling Luke but he didn't reply. We thought he'd got murdered.

We ran out of the house and rang the police on my mobile. I told them my friend's been kidnapped. They came as quick as they could and went into the house, checked it but said there was no one in it. I said, 'Did you check the loft?'

They said, 'No!'

Luke was in the loft tied up but the ghost had gone. They untied Luke, we were all fine.

But when my mum and dad got home, I got badly told off because they said, 'Don't open the door to anybody and don't watch any scary movies.' But other than that they said, 'We are glad you're OK, and no one got hurt.'

Kyle Connolly (11)
St Michael's Catholic High School, Watford

A Day Behind The Books

I was always a quiet girl, who would prefer to go to the school library and snuggle up into a book, than go outside and play with all the other children. It was hammering down outside, children sheltered inside the library. They would talk, rather than read a book, do their homework. The school librarian, Mrs Richards, was rather distressed because everyone thought she was too old to handle rowdy students; so, they took advantage of her. That's where Mr Jones came in ...

Mr Jones was mysterious. Didn't reveal anything. Say anything, and certainly take any nonsense. Anyway, it was on this day that I asked Mrs Richards if I could go somewhere quieter, like her office.

'Of course you can; but my office is busy. Listen. There's a small room upstairs on the left. It's quiet, sometimes students like you, go up there. It's a secret.'

I was galloping up the stairs so fast I'd forgotten what she had said, and went to the door on the right. I burst in, it was dark, cobwebs were everywhere. I found a small white chair, sat down and began to read. I started feeling dizzy, as if I were taller and fatter. I couldn't get off the chair and was stuck. I blinked. I was downstairs again, in the library. Suddenly, I could hear individual pupils speaking and gossiping. But what frightened me most was, when Mr Jones walked by he whispered, 'Afternoon Bookshelf.' That's where my fun began.

Charlotte Dormon (11)
St Michael's Catholic High School, Watford

The Old House Dare

It was Friday 13th and the middle of the night. Sally, Babz, Annie, Robby, Dave and I were walking around this old house that we'd dared to stay in for the night.

It was only when we were in a dark room and my flashlight went out, when we all got scared (me the most!) There were noises that didn't sound human.

The sounds got louder the things got nearer, we all screamed, the door slammed, we ran to the window and that was shut tight. We all huddled together and hoped that nothing would happen.

It came nearer and nearer, we ran to a corner. We saw something, and then looked away, when we looked back, it was gone. Robby and Dave went to see, but all they saw was a mouse, but I knew there was something else there.

The thing jumped out and we all screamed and looked back to find it was the four people that dared us trying to scare us. I can tell you it did! After that we all laughed about it.

I called my mum to pick us up, so we could tell our mates all about our adventure the next day.

Hannah Whitear (11)
St Michael's Catholic High School, Watford

A Day In the Life Of Eliza

I woke up. I got out of bed and staggered downstairs; I ate my breakfast and headed upstairs to get ready for school. I wore my pink Converses, I grabbed my bag and left.

'So Eliza, you ready for your big day?' said Jess.

'You must be so nervous, you have to ruin Daisy's reputation, and if you don't, you'll be embarrassing yourself and us.' Rosie spoke so casually like this was an ordinary day like any other.

Today I had to perform a dance off against Daisy Turnball at school, we'd be dancing to a mix by Danny in our form, and I was determined to win!

When we got to school, I went to the courts where Daisy was waiting; everyone in our year was sitting on the wall waiting for me. Daisy had her skirt hitched up like the rest of the girls. Danny was sitting with his CD player on his lap. The music started. I let Daisy start, and I stood in an intimidating pose. Daisy started dancing, she did the genie and then jumped back up again into a pose. It was my turn. I also did her genie sequence but better. I bent my legs and bobbed down, I got up and went back to my position.

Daisy jumped forward kicking her legs and stepping back. She stopped; she had run out of moves. I jumped into the splits, landed and brought myself back up to my pose and watched Daisy do some embarrassing disco moves. Daisy was furious! She went over to Danny, snatched his CD player and threw it on the ground.

How did I know how good this day would be?

Helen Byrne (12)
St Michael's Catholic High School, Watford

The Volcano Treasure

There was once a wizard and a knight who were very good friends. They trusted each other very well and were together every journey and adventure they went on.

When they were searching through a lot of old maps and legends, they came across a very interesting myth. This mythical story was about a long-lost treasure at the tropical island of Montana. In the very centre of this island was a very big volcano, probably one of the biggest volcanoes ever. They read on to find out that this volcano was the very place where the treasure was.

The wizard and the knight thought long and hard and came to a decision to set off on another very important journey to the tropical island of Montana.

A week later they arrived at the island of Montana. They travelled through many days and nights to get to the volcano. They travelled through hot and cold. When they got to the volcano, they looked up and thought, are we going to be able to do this? They were positive and said they could. They got all their gear out like their climbing boots, rope and their harnesses.

They climbed up the volcano and were getting weak and tired. Eventually they got to the top. The wizard lowered the knight down. The knight could see it. He reached out to grab it when the volcano exploded. They quickly saw the treasure melt. They failed, but thought there was more to money!

Sean Gower (12)
St Michael's Catholic High School, Watford

Who Is It?

I was about 14 years old and I got asked to babysit for my mum's friend. I replied yes, as you do! But what they did not know was I had never babysat for anyone before. I did not know what to do.

The next day when I arrived they told me where everything was; 'The cups are in the cupboard above the sink, the cutlery is in the drawer next to the sink, help yourself to the food, you know the rest.'

Finally when they left I put on a horror film. I don't know why because I hate them. When it was playing I was sat cuddled up in a ball, in the corner of the seat. Terrified when panic struck me, I was out of my mind watching the gory, outrageous horror film. When it finally finished I could not move, I completely froze. It was completely silent, it felt like ages, but it was only a few seconds before I could get up and go to the kitchen to make myself a drink. There was not a sound to be heard. Then the silence was suddenly broken, by the sound of footsteps upstairs.

At first I panicked, then I went slowly upstairs ...

Georgia Barnett (11)
St Michael's Catholic High School, Watford

Clown Attack

It was a Saturday morning in 18th century France when it happened.

As the le Fevre family were sitting down for dinner they could hear a moaning sound coming from the hall.

'Go and see what that terrible noise is will you Louis Junior?'

'Certainly, Mother,' replied Louis, so off he went to see what that noise was.

'Argh!' shouted Louis, his family came running in to see what all the shouting was about and there it was ... *the clown* standing over the body of one of the servants who had a knife in his chest. The clown had been haunting rich families through France for almost 100 years. The family were dumbstruck at the sight, the clown started towards them then with the bloody knife he had taken out of the servant,

'Quick, run, now,' shouted Monsieur le Fevre. The family started running but the clown just followed them wherever they went.

'We can't get rid of him,' shouted Louis Junior.

'Quick, this way,' shouted Maria.

The family ran up a flight of stairs towards the roof.

'What are we going to do here?' said Louis.

'Just watch,' said Maria, 'Maybe if we shout loud enough the fire brigade might come and rescue us.'

Just then they heard the door creak, they saw the clown standing there with his ghastly smile on his terrifying face. From behind them they heard a terrible groan, spinning around they saw their father and then ... all went black.

Tom Panayiotou (12)
St Michael's Catholic High School, Watford

An Unforgettable Experience

The van was packed with all our furniture, we were moving to the countryside.

When we were approaching the road leading to the house, suddenly all the lights in the street went out, all of a sudden there was a man standing in the road waving a lantern.

Dad got out of the car, the man came over, the man never spoke. He pointed to his left, there amongst the trees was a house, but only saw the shadow as it was a full moon on the night.

The man walked, so Dad, Mum, my sister, my brother and me followed. The man opened the door and stood back.

There was a very large hallway, there were candles lit as well. The rooms were dusty and cobwebs everywhere.

We stayed the night. It was hard to sleep. It was morning so we went back to the car, but the car was only feet away from the edge of a cliff.

When we looked back he had disappeared and so had the house, all that was there was a field.

Later Mum and Dad had found out that there had been a house years ago. A man, woman and child had lived there but the woman and child had been swept by the wind, the father tried to save them but he died too.

People say that when people get lost at night they appear along with the house and save lives.

Do you believe in ghosts?

Now I do.

Vanessa Nolan (12)
St Michael's Catholic High School, Watford

A Day In The Life Of Kobe Bryant

At the annual slam dunk competition, (a basketball game where players score by slamming the basketball down the hoop with their hands touching the hoop's rim), I watched all the other contestants do their dunks. I was thinking of mixing a dunk with a 360 degrees spin when I heard someone shout from the crowd saying, 'Someone should try through the legs while doing the 360 degrees.'

Brilliant idea!

I will do a 360 degree spin but followed by the windmill.

From their seats, the pros, Magic Johnson, Allen Iverson, Tracey McGrady and Jason Kidd gave me funny looks but I thought that they were just trying to look cool for the fans! I thought nothing of it. Some fans made posters saying 'If you mess with the best you'll end up like the rest! Kobe will wipe the floor with your faces!'

The judges signalled for me to start my dunk. My fans screamed, 'Kobe, Kobe, Kobe, Kobe ...' The chants were getting faster as I dribbled towards the net. I attempted the impossible; knowing that I might fail, I soared through the air while doing the 360 degree spin followed by the windmill. I had completed it! I hung on the hoop for extra points. While the pros and I were waiting for the scores; the results were ... in third place, Magic Johnson! ... Second place Shaquille O'Neil, first place ... Kobe Bryant! The fans roared with happiness, as I had won the competition for the third year running!

Edward Daniels (12)
St Michael's Catholic High School, Watford

The Reclaiming Of The Lost Land!

As the sun shone above the village, Captain Knightly and his exhausted army strolled into London town battered and bruised but with smirks on their faces as they had yet again won another battle in the west of Europe. They had come for supplies that they had used up in the battle and were very extremely low on. They went to the blacksmiths to collect swords and horseshoes. As they entered the blacksmiths the old, worried-looking man behind the counter stood up and asked Captain Knightly what he wanted.

'Can I have 30 swords and 50 horseshoes please,' replied Captain Knightly.

The man handed over the goods that he had requested. 'That will be 20 pieces of bronze please.'

As the captain was handing over his money he asked the man a question. 'What seems to be troubling you?'

'Well it's just the king is raising the taxes for everyone and we're all just trying to make ends meet for ourselves.'

'Anything I could help with?' suggested Captain Knightly.

'Oh no don't worry about me I'll be alright,' the old man replied as he limped into the corner.

'You know I could talk to the king about it, he only lives in the palace a couple of miles away.'

'Oh would you really!' the man shouted as he leapt up with joy. 'It would be great if you could!'

Captain Knightly took on the man's request and went outside to set off for the king's palace. As he did so there were many people standing there in the fog staring at him. They all looked like they were suffering and were aggrieved by the king. The captain pitied them, he shouted out to them, 'I will go to the king and debate with him about what he is doing with his people and country, and if necessary I will fight for the people of England.'

The crowd gave out a big roar, but what was next in store for the Captain and his army ... ?

Jason Burge (12)
St Michael's Catholic High School, Watford

A Letter To Myself

My name is Sally-Anne Liner, twenty-nine years of age I've got a wonderful husband and two children called Jake and Gemma. They are both wonderful.

Anyway, getting to the point, we just moved house two days ago, when I found a letter I had written to myself when I was twelve. I was in our new attic, the letter was in a box, I had brought with me.

I don't know how it got there, but when I read it, weird feelings came over me and then read it again ...

'Friday 17th May 1989

Dear Self,

Today is my birthday. I'm not at all happy even though you're supposed to feel happy on your birthday. Well today is different. I'll give you three reasons why:

Parents forget

No presents

No friends

Thank God today is Saturday. I can lock myself in my bedroom all day and sulk. What fun! I just hate my parents, really, they forget everything and I mean everything.

Birthdays for one, their own anniversary, getting me to school. They even forget me, their own daughter. Shocking I know. Not even a birthday cake. Boo hoo, they do apologise but sometimes sorry isn't good enough.

Next year 13, a teenager, let's see if my parents can remember that?

I doubt it.

Bye

Still hate them

Sally-Anne

xxx'.

At that moment memories came rushing back. That horrible day in the life of me. Nearly 30! Getting older as we speak.

Olivia Squires (12)
St Michael's Catholic High School, Watford

Risen

Tiffany opened the cathedral door. It was mahogany with gold detailing all the way around it. She stepped inside, her Gucci ballet shoes tapping on the black stone floor. She knew he would be waiting for her.

Tiffany stepped inside. She walked towards the altar, the organ began to play. She took off her shoes and looked up, there was a cross with Jesus on it above her head, and he was staring down at her.

She began to rise, her white nightgown billowing in the midnight breeze. Her long blonde hair delicately blowing in the midnight wind. She disappeared.

Tiffany was a bright girl; she was always going out with someone. She was rich and had her mates, and her enemies. She had all the latest designer gear. She was always having an argument with somebody.

'The mass has ended, go in peace.' The priest held up his hands as a sign of love. The family started to pour out of the cathedral.

The Sanders family decided to go for a walk after their morning at church. They wandered through the grassy fields. They laughed and sang jolly songs clambering up the hill until suddenly they saw Tiffany on the cross, her hands nailed to the wooden beam, her legs nailed onto a wooden block.

Their faces full of fear they stepped back … she had risen.

Tashauna Halligan (12)
St Michael's Catholic High School, Watford

Haunted

People think I'm weird because I hear voices. I started hearing them when we moved into a new house about four years ago when I was nine. My name's Cornelius Fletcher, I live alone with my big sister Katie in a small house in the middle of nowhere. I hate my school, I hate everything about it.

My sister is twenty-six, has an OK job which is enough to provide us with food and school stuff. She also hears the voices. There's something about our house, something supernatural that we have never looked into because we're too terrified of what we might find. Over the last three days the voices are becoming more persistent and more threatening.

I got home one afternoon and my sister wasn't at home. I was a bit worried. I knew she should be back by now. 'Katie, you there?' I shouted. I heard a soft creaking sound at the end of the hall and standing there in the doorway of the bathroom was a boy, dead and rotting. I screamed, 'Where's Katie, what have you done?'

He replied softly, 'Will you be my brother?'

I was trembling but instinct told me to go into the bathroom so I did and lying in the bath was my sister, dead. I screamed at the boy, 'What have you done you warped freak?'

He said, 'I can bring her back if you'll be my brother.'

'OK, OK, I'll be your brother,' I said.

Then he smiled softly, Katie woke up and the boy was gone. We never heard the voices again.

Jack Townsend (12)
St Michael's Catholic High School, Watford

Letter Kidnapper

Polly had an excruciating day at school but was that the end of it? Since she recently broke up with Thomas most things were going wrong. She didn't know what to do. Was there a spot on her face or maybe people just had a grudge against her? It made her feel uncomfortable the way people looked at her.

The next day, she woke up with an immensely bad headache. Polly had also had a bad dream the night before. She did not want to go to school but her mum had forced her to.

A few minutes after Polly had left the house to make her way to school, a man approached her and asked her for directions to the nearest post box. As the post box was on the way to school, Polly took the man with her. But when she reached the end of the road, she had to go through an alleyway. The man had taken Polly on a detour down another lane which was heading in the completely wrong direction of school and the post box.

But the thing that Polly noticed at first was that when the man asked for directions, he didn't seem to have any letter or package to send away. When she had realised that he was kidnapping her, she started to scream for help. 'Argh! Help me I'm being kid-' and then her words were ended by a spine-shivering gunshot. That was going to cure her appalling headache ...

Katie Ross (12)
St Michael's Catholic High School, Watford

How Monkeys Got Into St Michael's Cave

When we went to Spain we were told about a cave on a place called Gibraltar. This cave was called St Michael's cave. We were told that there were some monkeys on Gibraltar that had come from Africa and that they lived on the side of Gibraltar. My dad said we should go and see and that's what we did in a car from our hotel.

When we got there they were right, it was a big rock sticking out of the sea. When we got to the main bit of the town my dad hired a taxi, which was like a mini bus to take us round.

The man drove us up the big rock telling us all about the history and he took us to St Michael's cave and we went in. The man told us that in a little while we would see the monkeys that were famous on the rock. He said the monkeys were apes and that they came from Africa. The legend says that St Michael's cave was so deep and long it stretched across the sea to Africa and the monkeys came that way.

The strange thing was that no one ever found a dead monkey on the rock, he said the other monkeys took the dead ones back through the cave to Africa or perhaps their ghosts lived in the cave but he didn't know.

It was really dark, there were lots of different shapes and shadows. I heard funny noises when we got to the darkest bit at the bottom, I heard a scraping noise and I got worried. My brother made me jump by saying 'monkey' and pointing behind me. I got out of the cave as fast as I could.

On some fencing was a big brown monkey and it was looking at me so I ran into the shop. My brother came out and he saw the monkey and was scared. We drove along a bit to another place where there were lots of monkeys and they jumped on our car, the man fed them.

A monkey jumped on my dad's shoulder and he gave the monkey some peanuts. One jumped on my brother, the man tried to get it off but it wouldn't let go of his hair and he got scared. In the end it got off but I laughed at my brother who had scared me in the cave but the real monkey scared him.

In the end I wasn't scared, and fed the oldest monkey, called Michael, if you said 'Give me five' he would touch your hand and then you gave him a peanut. Then we went back to the hotel and laughed all about it.

Michael Mottershead (11)
St Michael's Catholic High School, Watford

The Hook

'And then,' Jack whispered, eyes wide with horror as his face shone in the moonlight, 'a tap, tap, tap on the window,' Jack continued as the boys leaned in closer. 'A creak, creak, creak from behind the door and as the door slowly opened, it struck 12 somewhere in the distance!' He exclaimed in excitement. 'As the figure swept across the room, the old lady noticed the sharp hook aimed for her heart, and she never heard a clock strike 12 again!' Jack finished.

'So, gory details please!' Scott quizzed.

'I dunno! That's all I was told,' Jack replied.

'Jack, is that a real story?' asked Scott's younger brother Kieran.

'No! Don't be stupid!' Jack laughed.

His laughter echoed round the dull deserted cemetery. It was a cold night in the Christmas holidays. The cemetery was full of atmosphere. The dull tombstones, the old, sad, overgrown trees, the creaky gates, the deserted church all made it seem like the perfect scene from a horror movie and a great place to tell spooky stories!

A clock struck 12 somewhere in the distance, the wind whistled, and a loud scream sounded through the cemetery. *Drip, drip, drip.* The boys looked up to see a silver hook hanging in the tree above their heads glinting with blood.

And Kieran never heard a clock strike 12 again.

Chloe O'Sullivan (12)
St Michael's Catholic High School, Watford

Four Is The Secret Number

Ring, ring, 'Hello police,' answered PC Wilson.

'There has been a stabbing at Stanley Park,' replied the unknown man. He then put down the phone.

The police drove as quickly as they could to Stanley park, where they saw a middle-aged man lying on the floor. The police investigated this incident for a while and tried to find out why the man who rang the police put the phone down straightaway, and withheld his number, but during the fourth day whilst they were investigating it, the police received another phone call saying there had been another stabbing in Hornets Park.

The police hurried off to the scene of the crime where they found another middle-aged man lying on the floor. The police investigated this incident as well but they couldn't find any evidence. But then on the fourth day the police received another phone call saying there had been another stabbing at King's Park. So the police went to the incident and found a teenager on the floor, they investigated it, and decided to see if there were any connections between the three stabbings. They noticed that each person had four stab wounds, all the stabbings happened four miles apart and all the phone calls were received at 4pm. So because of this the police expected there to be a fourth stabbing four miles away. Four days after the stabbings at King's Park. And there was. The stabber was caught.

Conor Carney (12)
St Michael's Catholic High School, Watford

Lost Visions

'Ooooo,' the howling of the wind ... I hear distant cries, my heart beats faster and faster and faster, a single drop of sweat slips down my forehead, I am getting so hot now and I am too afraid to move ... 'Help!' the light flickers and then turns on, to my relief it's only Mum and Dad.

'Honey, what is the matter?' says my half-asleep Mum.

'Nothing, just a bad dream,' the door closes and I am left alone ...

I have been having a lot of scary dreams ever since I moved house. Mainly of a translucent old lady cradling a baby, crying. This house used to be my grandmother's and I asked her if it was haunted and she said that her great, great grandmother used to live there and one of her daughters had a rare illness, but her mum thought she was dead and committed suicide, but her daughter grew up and had a proper family.

I tried to tell the ghost but she wouldn't listen, and she kept crying and holding her baby. I felt the heat of anger build up inside me. I got more and more frustrated and then I snapped. I took my clenched fist and threw it at her face and surprisingly, I felt the impact. Then I took her baby and showed her she's still alive, but then she screamed so loud, I suddenly jumped right of my bed only to find it was another bad dream ...

Marisa Scannell (12)
St Michael's Catholic High School, Watford

Cassandra's Story

Aloha! My name is Cassandra Duvalia and I live in Haleiwa, Oahu, Hawaii. I have to tell someone about this crazy escapade even though you will think 'Pupule!' Oh, sorry, I keep forgetting you aren't Hawaiian. The world 'Pupule' means either 'crazy' or 'you're crazy'. OK? You all got that? Even the little ones? All right let's move ahead!

The day began like any other. You know, get up, brush hair, get dressed, have breakfast, clean teeth, etc. Then I walked down to the beach with my surfboard and bag. I saw my mate in the sea and so I went to join her. As soon as I saw her up close, then I realised something was wrong. As in really wrong! Her normally deep brown eyes were sort of white and misted over.

Suddenly, she made a grab for me and pulled me under the water. Next thing I knew I was on the beach and felt really dizzy when there was a sudden flash of bright light and I saw a parade of men going by and destroying the town. I realised this was the future and ran back to town. I warned the sellers and they fled. Next I realised what had happened to my friend. The men must have known I would see this and had bewitched my friend to drown me so they could destroy the town and be in power. So believe this if you like but I don't care. See you soon. Aloha!

Cassandra.

Eleanor Nutkins (12)
St Michael's Catholic High School, Watford

Cotswold Cemetery

On a brisk, rainy evening Lola was cycling home from school. Every evening on her way home she passed an old cemetery, with old gnarled trees which hung down like evil spirits looming over you. She had heard many rumours about the cemetery in the school playground.

Lola turned her neck round so that she could take a peek at the cemetery. But on this particular night, the brakes on her bike stopped as if they had a mind of their own. Her feet were marching her towards the iron gates and she couldn't stop. The gates creaked open and Lola stepped inside.

Her feet kept moving never stopping. In the distance she could make out a tombstone with the name Marion Maskion on it. She heard a piercing scream. She spun around and standing behind her was a woman with no head screaming and using her razor-sharp eyes to transfix Lola. The trees came closer to her and their branches turned into figures which were ready to grab something, or someone!

'Help!' screamed Lola, but she knew nobody could hear. She tried to back away but she bashed into a tombstone.

'Somebody help me!'

Then the moon started to disappear as morning was breaking and the Headless Lady completely vanished, the trees went back to being trees. Lola ran as fast as possible to her bike, grabbed it and cycled home and she hoped she would never have to pass the cemetery again.

Jessica Fuller (12)
St Michael's Catholic High School, Watford

The Haunted Mansion

Becky lived with her dad; they were very close and would have fun together.

Anyway …

One day during break at school, Becky's friend Sophie dared her to go in the forest and stay for one hour in the Haunted Mansion on the hill.

'OK I'll do it,' replied Becky.

That night Becky lied to her dad and said that she was going to stay at Sophie's but instead she went to the Haunted Mansion.

When Becky got to the mansion, she heard these strange and weird noises through the door. She was terrified. She rang the doorbell. The door opened. Wherever Becky looked there were bones scattered, even full skeletons!

On every pillar in every corner there were cobwebs and spiders.

Becky saw loads of shadows in the moonlight.

One was coming towards her. Nearer and nearer …

'Boo!' A frail old man scared the living daylights out of Becky.

She had never met a man who felt so evil but looked so nice and sweet!

He invited her to sit down. So she did!

'I'm sorry about all these bones,' he said. 'I just couldn't help it, they all looked so yummy, I just had to eat them all!'

'Argh!' screamed Becky as she ran out of the mansion.

'Dad, Dad!'

'What is it? I've been worried sick. Where have you been?'

'I've been at the Haunted Mansion,' she babbled.

'Calm down. Come inside and tell me all about it.'

Amy Lovell (12)
St Michael's Catholic High School, Watford

The Room

The door creaked open. The darkness blinds your eyes, you cannot see anything except a small light far away. You hear a crash behind you as the door slammed close. You think how you loved the sunlight, and start walking for the far twilight. Every step you take, you hear a creak of the floorboard. You hear whispers in the shadows. You smell a rotten fish hanging on the ceiling.

The window far, opens and a blast of wind come and sweep you on the floor. Suddenly your hair stands as a hand creeps onto your shoulder. You hear a dripping sound and you look down and there on your T-shirt shiny red blood. You try to run but can't move. While you try, the scream of cackles ring in your ears. A light shines through your back and light starts to cover the place and you hear the familiar voice of a friend. The weight that was once on your shoulder disappears and you turn around and see the light.

Geneva Mayuga (11)
St Michael's Catholic High School, Watford

One World

Cinderella, Sleeping Beauty and Jasmine were getting ready for their premiere of their new film 'One World' when the phone rang.

Jasmine jumped up hysterically, hoping it would be one of the boys.

'Hello?' Jasmine said. 'Oh it's you Belle!' she said disappointedly.

'I hope Batman is going to be there!' Sleep says.

'Yeah, I hope so too, he's buff!' Cinderella said, shyly.

Jasmine came off the phone and explained that Belle was going to pick them up at 8pm.

The girls looked lovely and were putting their make-up on, however the boys hadn't got a clue. Prince Charming was messing with his hair; beast was looking for his shoes and Aladdin was just in a flap.

'Shall I take the genie lamp just in case we need some advice when we chat up the girls?' Aladdin asked.

'Yeah, whatever, but I'm good at that already!' Prince answered.

Hours passed and all seven of them left in the limo.

When they turned up at the premiere, Cinderella and Prince Charming strolled down the red carpet hand in hand. Jasmine and Aladdin were close behind, followed by Belle and Beast and then there was Sleeping Beauty alone. It was at that moment when they realised something was wrong. Sleep's dreams were about to be shattered, it was Shrek at the door, not Batman. They had gone to the wrong premiere, wrong night.

'What's the point of having a genie when you're always forgetting him?' Beast said angrily to Aladdin.

Brodie O'Shea (12)
St Michael's Catholic High School, Watford

Trapped

I walked up the stairs of the old house on the hill. I looked at it with its broken windows, muddy path and dark surroundings. I turned to my friends and they made a 'go on!' motion with their hands. I took one last look, before I knocked on the front door. It was made of old wood and the paint was peeling. I waited for about ten seconds before I stepped down, the house was obviously empty. I breathed a sigh of relief, but I was about to walk back down when the door opened quickly, but there was no one there. For some reason, I felt pulled into the house, to see what was in there and what was to be discovered inside this building that was forgotten by the rest of the world. I entered, knowing I shouldn't, but nevertheless I walked in.

As I walked in I felt a chill down my back and I gulped as I saw the mysterious shadows looming in the background. The carpet was tatty, and the walls were an unfriendly shade of yellow, the darkness everywhere. Then something … or someone ran across the landing, but my eyes were not quick enough to see it. I knew I should get out. Now. But I turned for the door, it was closed. I attempted to open it but it was tightly shut. I was trapped.

Fiona Burke (12)
St Michael's Catholic High School, Watford

Blade Quadrent

25 years ago back in New York, Drago, leader of all vampires, was awoken by non-day walkers. In the end Blade defeated him and was never seen again … until now.

But Drago wasn't the only one that returned. Drake returned too. But this time they're more mad, and stronger than ever.

In Los Angeles, Blade sensed something bad, something real bad. He sensed that Drago and Drake have risen, but what he wanted to know was how?

He left his hideout as soon as he could and ran to where his carer's daughter's hideout was, and he told her what he sensed. She couldn't believe it, because she was there when Drago was killed, and she was told about Drake's death when she was a little girl.

A few days later, Blade was walking down the street, when he sensed Dragon and Drake's presence, but the thing was that it was scattered … and then he saw them, on top of a business building, but they weren't alone. Dragon and Drake were holding men and women from the inside of the building, and holding them over the edge.

Blade ran and ran all the way to the top of the building, but it was too late. Drago and Drake were gone … and so were the citizens.

He told what happened on the street to his daughter Abbie and she was shocked. She told him that it wasn't his fault.

To be continued … or is it?

Kyle Quaye (11)
St Michael's Catholic High School, Watford

Untitled

I was carried in as my breath was taken away by the smell of toxics slightly travelling up my throat. There were many people stuffed around in this squashed room I had been taken into. The loud music vibrated into my eardrums as soon as I walked in. I was carried on further as I was jolted by people moving around, hard enough that my dummy fell out. People were shouting over each other all around the room. People were sitting holding some kind of glass that would sometimes touch their lips.

My mum placed me on a seat next to my dad and went off to some kind of wood object where they were handing out the glass objects others were holding. Suddenly the noise rose and so did everyone jump to their feet shouting and screaming. They were pointing and shouting at some kind of coloured screen. They stopped screaming but carried on with their eyes glued to the screen, that was when I knew it was safe so I drifted slowly off to sleep.

Amy Jenkins (13)
St Michael's Catholic High School, Watford

Why Me?

I woke up to glorious sunshine; little did I know the horrors waiting for me that dreadful morning. I dressed hurriedly, ate a good breakfast and left the house with confidence.

I arrived, turned the corner to find Terror staring back at me. I closed my eyes hoping to block out all the horrors that I knew were waiting for me. Screams echoed from every angle as I was plunged into darkness. I was jolted back and forth, unable to see. All my limbs were out of control, it was up to them now, there was no going back. Why did I let myself into this? Why did I risk everything that I have?

Up ahead I saw a ghostly figure swaying from side to side. I heard eerie moaning coming from beneath my feet. Something clammy touched my face. There was deadly silence. Everything was black. I felt breath down my neck. The screaming started again and malicious laughter echoed in my ears. I couldn't bear it, would this nightmare never end? I closed my eyes as I felt my body hurtle forward again. I couldn't breathe and with a sudden jolt of my body I was greeted by a foul headless ghoul. I froze. His breath was unbearably hot. He laughed one last terrible laugh and with a last scream I was hurtled forward to be greeted by the joys of daylight and warm sunshine on my face. My ride on the ghost train was over. Never again.

Erin Oakley (13)
St Michael's Catholic High School, Watford

Racing Back In Time ...

'Brittney?' called an unrecognisable voice. I rubbed my eyes and woke to find myself lying in bed in a hotel. I looked up; a younger girl was looking at me frowning. I jumped out of bed.

'Brittney! It's me, Amy, your personal trainer!'

Trainer? I thought, confused.

'Come on, you'd better hurry, you'll be late for the 2012 Olympics!'

'2012 Olympics?'

'Yes! It's your big race!' She sighed and rolled her eyes.

'I can't run to save my life, let alone for Great Britain!' I muttered to myself.

She handed me skin tight shorts and a stripy vest. 'Hurry up, you've overslept. You're acting really strange!' Amy shouted anxiously. I laughed, *people in 2012 are very uptight!* I thought to myself.

On the way to the stadium I noticed how things were different compared with 3013. The cars were strangely shaped, the houses were made of brick and the people wore tracksuits ... funny-looking outfits!

'On your marks ... set ...' the gunshot went and I was off, running swiftly round the bend. I reached the next lap and picked up pace. Breathing breathlessly round the bend again, the others close by. At the last hundred metres I sprinted like a greyhound to the finish but it was too close to call.

I waited patiently for the results. 'The winner is ... Brittney Black!' I was flabbergasted and Amy couldn't stop squealing with excitement. It was such an amazing experience, words couldn't describe my day back in time.

Laura Graham (13)
St Michael's Catholic High School, Watford

A Ghost Story

Long, long ago in a quiet village called Sleepy Hollow, there was a big mansion where a middle-class man lived with his old mother who was 83 years old.

One foggy night Mr Campbell heard a noise up in his attic and went to investigate. Mr Campbell could not remember where he'd left his ladder, so he decided to have a look in his garage. As he approached his garage door he noticed that it was open, he went inside and spotted a torch in its wrong place. The torch was also still on. The torch was on his table where he was designing a sign. The sign was gone.

Then a man wearing a black tracksuit with a hood, walked into his garage behind. The man hit Mr Campbell on the back of his head with a crowbar. The man ran off with the sign but while he was running away he dropped the crowbar in the grass beside him. Mr Campbell was lying there hopelessly very still on the floor, and he slowly drifted into a coma.

Two days later …

Mrs Campbell phoned the police to tell them that her son was missing. The police arrived. One of the policemen saw someone lying on the garage floor in a pool of blood. Mrs Campbell was put in a care home because she was too old to look after herself, and the mansion was sold to the man in the black suit (Mr Tweedy), but three years later Mr Campbell's spirit finally helped the punishment for the murder of Mr Campbell.

Mr Tweedy got so scared he killed himself. Mr Campbell's spirit is still in the house this day …

Sean McNally
St Michael's Catholic High School, Watford

The Woods

'Hello,' he said. I couldn't see him, I couldn't see anything, I was trapped in darkness.

'Who are you, what do you want? Let me go!' I screamed.

He replied, 'I'm warning you of a grave danger if you go to the woods tonight.'

'What's going to happen to me? Tell me!' I shouted over and over again.

The voice said, 'I can't tell you but I can show you.' A yellow flash suddenly shot out from the ground and I fell into it. And I thought it was the end.

I can't remember falling onto the cold, damp surface of the woods and I can't remember falling through the vortex. But I was here now and I had to find out what was happening. My life depended on it. I was wearing a rucksack. As I remember packing my bag, I put a torch into the left hand pocket and reached for it. I found it and started walking again I reached the tatty green tents and a flat stony patch of ground. Suddenly I heard a tree twig snap, I heard a rustle and a tree branch snap, I turned around and he jumped at me …

Nathan Dunton (12)
St Michael's Catholic High School, Watford

Lost Souls

Annabelle, a blonde bubbly character who loved the catwalk, her boyfriend, Luke was a shorthaired brunette who longed to be in the Olympics doing pole-vault. Amy was a beautiful, smart, talented redhead with luscious hair and rosy cheeks. I had always desperately wanted to be a part of the gang ... my mistake.

My initiation night. The old church had been abandoned for years now, no one had been in there, leaving it as the perfect place for the ceremony.

We were all dressed in black and red robes (actually they were more like tea towels), standing in front of the altar in a circle with me standing in the centre with a candle.

Luke started talking in what he thought was an eerie voice. 'Come unto us oh Lucifer my lord and welcome this boy into our group. At that point everything flew backwards, bursting through the already crumbling back wall. All four of us jumped up in horror to greet a small man with what seemed to look like horns coming out of his head.

'You rang! Now all you have to do is sign this contract, um I mean this blank piece of paper to say that you're in the gang.' He thrust a piece of paper in front of our noses, the other three looked as puzzled as I did and then stupidly, we all signed it.

And now here I am, in this hellhole. I had had a few uninvited and unwanted visitors over the past few days. One of them taunted me, one of whom I recognised.

'Where are your friends now? Oh yes, I remember, the 'accidents'. Poor Luke it was his big break, he would have been an Olympic gold medallist but oh dear, the pole snapped. What with all that blood pouring from his wounds, his limp body just hung there. How Annabelle screamed. Yes, yes, yes, Annabelle the model, it was such a waste of a life, if only there wasn't a gap in the stage.' He sniggered. 'She was crumpled to death, her screams for help just wasted her breath. And what of Amy, strangled to death by a wire. All three accidents you were there, all three of them you were accused of. But now you won't be accused of anything, you won't see any more deaths, apart from your own. After all, I'm the Devil's minion and you did sell me your soul.'

Luisa Beeken (13)
St Michael's Catholic High School, Watford

The Beauty Pageant

Sarah would do anything to get her own way.

She was walking through the corridor of her school. She walked past the bulletin board. She doesn't normally read anything on it, but something caught her eye, it read: *Beauty Pageant Sign Here.* She just had to enter, she was sure she would win. She got out a pen and put her name down. 'Let's see which losers have signed up for here,' she said to herself, she looked down the list to see her competition, well lack of anyway. She got a sudden shock when she saw a name she recognised. Her best friend Lisa had entered the competition. She was angry so she went to confront her on the way home from school.

'How can you do this to me? I thought we were friends,' Sarah said, basically shouting.

'It's a free country, I can do whatever I want!' Lisa said back.

'Yeah, well you could have told me.'

'You're just jealous of the competition.'

'Hardly.'

'Let's just see who wins shall we?' and Lisa stormed off.

A few weeks later, Sarah and Lisa were finalists in the beauty pageant. Saran went up to Lisa to wish her good luck. 'Hey want a drink?'

'Sure,' Sarah handed her a cup of orange, she drank it quickly. Then it was Sarah's turn to go on stage, everyone cheered as she went off. She went backstage and saw everyone crying. Lisa had suddenly collapsed.

Sarah won the beauty pageant ...

Tasha Msanide (13)
St Michael's Catholic High School, Watford

Ghost Story

Tom, Bill and their parents were just packing the last few things because they were moving house. They were moving to a big house on its own, but they didn't know the house was haunted, or that a family had died in it during the Second World War, and they haunt the house.

Later that day, they arrived at their house and they started taking all their things in.

The next day they started unpacking their stuff. They put some boxes in the hallway then, an hour later, they were back next to the front door.

Later that day they went to sleep. Then when they woke up and went downstairs, everything was packed and put next to the front door. They went downstairs into the basement and then the door slammed shut and the light was flashing on, off, on, off. They tried to open the door but it was locked. They heard a voice saying, 'You will not get out of this house alive!'

Then Tom's Dad smashed the door down!

Michael O'Toole (12)
St Michael's Catholic High School, Watford

The Minotaur

We were in the cave and the chase was on, my dragon slayer was clenched tightly in my hand.

We were looking, keeping every move stealthy, the wall opened. Lernargh my trusty fellow archer had his magic longbow at the ready. We went in and a moss giant came out of the gooo! Lernargh shot him in the head with a mituril fire arrow. We ran, we saw our worst fear on the trip to the Minotaur.

We yelled and jumped off the edge onto an unsteady path leading to a small cave. The Minotaur gave a mighty roar, we hid on a split bark trunk.

The pressure was on, *smash!* The Minotaur's head fell off. Lernargh shot him with an arrow.

We had won the battle, the city was safe.

I was getting tired, so I turned off Runescape and the computer, I went downstairs and fell asleep.

Jack Dorgan (11)
St Michael's Catholic High School, Watford

Untitled

'We've eaten too much popcorn.'

'No *you've* eaten too much popcorn.'

It was turning 1 o'clock and Chloe and her friends were only just going to bed, it was going to be an exciting sleepover.

Sasha, Stevie and Christina fell asleep, but Chloe didn't. She couldn't get to sleep and she was worried something awful was going to happen.

Creak went the floorboards. Chloe shivered. 'Who's there?' she muttered. Nobody answered. Suddenly a white slithery creature appeared in front of her. It grabbed Chloe and took her off.

'Where's Chloe?' asked Sasha in the morning.

'She must have gone downstairs,' replied Stevie.

Sasha, Stevie and Christina went downstairs but Chloe was nowhere to be seen.

'Chloe goes to the graveyard when she's sad,' Christina mumbled.

It was silent in the graveyard. It was pitch-black. 'What's that?' Stevie pointed at a creature.

'Erm … a demon!' shouted Sasha.

The group of girls figured out that it was guarding something, but what could it be?

'Help!' shouted a tired voice. 'Help! Sasha, Stevie, Christina help!'

Chloe! they all thought at once.

Christina ran to Chloe's house and got a knife. When she returned Stevie was punching the creature and Sasha did a backflip, as she was a fantastic gymnast. Christina stabbed the creature, it fell to the floor. Chloe was stuck down a deep hole but Sasha found a rope and pulled her out.

After that nobody ever saw the demon again.

Heidi Currid (12)
St Michael's Catholic High School, Watford

The Death Of Daisy Barker!

It was Friday the 13th, tonight I had been invited out for a meal with my boyfriend. I had to straighten my hair and sort out my outfit.

It was getting dark and menacing. I lived alone in a humungous mansion down in Dorset. I was placed between overgrown weeds and thousands of trees. At night you could hear repeated screams of what sounded like dead people. The thought that scared me was the fact that their bodies would fly amongst my house and haunt me in my sleep.

I was sitting at my posh, fancy dressing table, straightening my hair. It was 11.30pm. I heard a dreadful scream, I knew it wasn't my mind playing tricks on me because I'd heard exactly the same scream earlier. I was petrified. I heard a rustle which sounded like someone was there. I legged it out of my room. Then the next minute someone in a black balaclava, obnoxiously slit something sharp, pointy, prickly and long right through my soft, smooth skin which caused me to scream and fall to the ground.

By the next day everybody knew what had happened. It was on the news straightaway in every country, thousands of people were trying to find my stranded body. Luckily someone found it, it was found at the very bottom of my pitch-black cellar down in the basement, my body was hidden in a big black dustbin liner …

Charlotte Gomez (12)
St Michael's Catholic High School, Watford

Myths And Legends

(An extract)

They say she died there. Through no fault of her own. But no one really knew the true, full story. A misty figure of a woman stands there overlooking the ocean. Why does she haunt the place and scare people? The legend has it she was killed there a long time ago and is still there living the horror, but why does she scare the living daylights out of every person to visit or dive past?

I was having a great time, the weather was pretty nice, the new people and just the great atmosphere the place had. I had never been to the beautiful beaches of Cornwall. I didn't know England had such nice places. We went out on the Tuesday, down to Newquay and spent the day roaming the streets, eating and looking in shops. The day went quickly. It was getting dark already. The place was so full of lots of colours and people, it was lively and fun. But at night it looked so different, so mysterious. I went down onto the beach; it was so pretty the sky was very dark blue almost black with a bright yellow moon floating in it. The moon made the dark water of the ocean glisten and sparkle. I sat there looking at the huge darkness. I liked it there, it was so peaceful and calm. I felt like I could be the only one on the Earth, there was no sound anywhere, just the ocean lapping against the shore. I looked around up to the high ocean walls that almost surrounded me, but it wasn't a treating feeling just one that made me wonder.

A shadow I saw at the corner made me lose concentration. I began to look around. But there was nothing. So I carried on thinking, when I could have sworn I saw a figure walk past. This scared me a bit; I looked around trying to find out what was near me, but still there was nothing there. I knew I'd seen something I was sure of it. Then about eight metres from me I saw this misty faint figure. I tried looking closer but it was pretty dark, I could only just see it from the glare of the moon. I stood up. It seemed to be drawing me towards it, my feet didn't really want me to go over there but they still kept moving closer. I couldn't turn back. My feet wouldn't stop. It was so near me. I closed my eyes. I could feel it breathing on me. I stood dead still frozen, scared to move. 'Open your eyes,' this weird kind of gentle voice said to me. I still couldn't though. It was still breathing on me. Cold long breaths of air, no smell to them just cold.

Then I slowly opened my eyes except I couldn't really see a face, there was a figure of a face but you couldn't quite see the details of it, and the eyes were faded. It sounds so strange but I can't really describe it. It wasn't like a real person there more like a presence, it was transparent because I could still see the sand and the darkness through it. Then it touched my shoulder ...

Danielle McAuley (15)
St Michael's Catholic High School, Watford

A Ghost Story

(An extract)

It wasn't until I heard the 'thump' of the cupboard door, the shatter of the heads of my china doll, the whispers of young children, the bitter breeze sending shivers downwards to my spine, that I realised I wasn't alone.

I put off the fact that supernatural events were happening all around me. I used to think it was my imagination playing tricks on me, well that's what my friends told me. It wasn't until the middle of last night, that I began to hear bizarre noises, of a little girl howling. I thought I was dreaming. I must have been, so I went back to bed, into the warmth of my cover where I felt protected from my dream that I was positive I was having. The cries got louder and they felt that if they were getting closer, this was no way my imagination. I pulled the covers firmly over my ears to drain the cries out, I felt safe being sheltered by my covers, I was no way safe.

It wasn't until I peered my head out of my cover that I realised the cries had stopped. I was grateful.

As I laid in my bed wondering what those cries were and who from, I took a glimpse and my beautiful china doll which I had got from my five-year-old cousin, which I adored as it was so striking, I noticed that the doll appeared to be glancing in my direction, it wasn't until I saw the doll fall from my wardrobe and shatter, that I started to hear thumping, and whispers from a young child. A chilling breeze went straight through me, I wasn't alone. To feel as if someone is watching you, watching every move you make, is so frightening, very gradually and silently, I peered over my bed to find a young girl weeping blood from her eyes, looking in my direction, to slowly see her move in a jagged way towards my bed which seemed to make me feel protected. I pulled the cover over my head. Each time I glanced out from my protection she was getting closer and closer. The air was getting colder and colder as she was coming closer, she wasn't living.

Abbi-Louise Wright (15)
St Michael's Catholic High School, Watford

A Day In The Life Of Nelson's Column

Standing here, tall and proud. In the centre of London. Watching the days go by. Seasons coming and going. Unsheltered from Mother Nature's decaying strength.

The things I see, the things I hear, stories I could tell, all throughout the ages, that no one else will ever know.

Some people think, that my presence, being in the centre of London and all, would mean that I would never be lonely. So many people looking at me, taking pictures, tourists talking to me, even Londoners eating their lunches by my 'Grand Presence'. But it's not like that. I feel lonely, not even being able to talk, smile, things that people take for granted. My eyes dead set in looking in one direction, never blinking, always staring. But the only part of me that's still working, are my ears. Listening to secrets untold. Plots. Promises. Revenge.

Standing here for so many years, I have watched generation after generation coming before me and growing up with newborn babies, talking about my heroic actions, saving the country and innocent people from dying.

As I stand here day to day I hear different variations of my 'life story'. Sometimes, in my head, I laugh, some of the things that they come out with are absurd.

So, here I stand. Tall and proud. Keeping secrets that won't see the light of day for many, many years. Still listening, thinking, watching and waiting. For my time to die again.

Charlotte Parker (14)
St Michael's Catholic High School, Watford

My Life As A Princess

I was living the dream of every 10-year-old girl in the world; it was the perfect life I have always dreamed of, ever since I was a little girl. Dressing up and not being me, but being someone every little girl wants to be. Wearing a beautiful pink puffy out dress with sequins and diamonds embroidered into it, with my curly brunette hair all flowing down with my diamond tiara on, and the rays of the sun reflecting on it as I ran after the white butterfly in the palace grounds.

Inside my palace, eating my banquet on my banqueting table of royal silver platters I began eating my golden chicken nuggets and French fries. I had to eat it all up, or I wouldn't be able to eat my pink fairy cakes after, and they were delicious.

My pink four-poster bed covered with diamonds, fairy lights and teddies all over the mattress which is like a big soft bouncy castle. The carpet is so deep that your feet get lost in the texture of it. It feels like having your feet in the clouds but knowing that you cannot fall. The mirrors have covered my pink walls, they are so complimenting to me, and I always look gorgeous when I look in my reflection.

Sneaking into the queen's dressing room is naughty, but I blame it on the maids all the time. I slither in and take a seat on the royal red throne and try on her diamonds and red rubies and her luscious pink lipstick, she only wears for best.

I'm all ready now to go and find my Prince Charming.

'I'm ready. I can't see you.'

Well I can dream of being a princess ... can't I?

Aisling Carney (15)
St Michael's Catholic High School, Watford

Short Story

All of a sudden I awoke in a hot, dark, eerie room, chained to a metal table, unable to move. After a while my body started to ache, suddenly I realised I had cuts and bruises all over my body.

It was late Friday evening and I was walking home through the fields after spending the evening with my friends. Somehow I managed to walk off the track and got myself lost. It was pitch-black. I couldn't see a thing then I fell. I hit my head on a stone and then I got knocked out. I awoke some time later, I tried to get up, but there was immense pain from my ankle, I knew straightaway that it was broken. I got my phone out of my pocket but it was crushed because I had fallen on it.

After about an hour I heard noises in the sky, and then I saw it, a big bright red light! I sat there for about a minute looking at it in amazement, then it started coming closer and closer. Then a figure from nowhere appeared, it got closer to me, it had some kind of injection with it, then all of a sudden it stabbed me with it and I fainted.

That is how I got myself in this room chained to a metal table. I don't know what is going to happen to me, whether I live or die. but I've got to go, someone is coming to torture me more, no doubt!

Jade Cook
St Michael's Catholic High School, Watford

A Night In The School

(An extract)

It was the day before our school was holding their annual musical, this year it was going to be 'Grease'. Hannah, Charlotte, Michael, Luke, Max and I volunteered to help set up the hall with the props. Mr Sheppard was meant to be directing us on where to put all the props, but instead went to McDonald's to get us some food. He had been gone for an hour and McDonald's was only a short walk away, down the road. What was taking him so long? We were so hungry that we started to explore the school for some snacks.

Earlier that day we had heard rumours about tonight. Tonight being the night that the ghost of the evil sister who built the school would walk the halls, and would terrorise any human who crossed her path. I did not believe it myself and neither did the others, so that's why we had volunteered because no one else would as they were too scared.

We split up into pairs; Michael and I checked the teacher's staffroom because they usually had lots of delicious snacks hidden away. Hannah and Luke went directly to the kitchen, as there would definitely be food in there. Charlotte and Max walked around the school checking each and every classroom for snacks. We had walkie talkies so that we could keep in constant contact with each other, just in case anything 'strange' happened. It did creep at the back of my mind that something might happen tonight … or maybe I was just starting to believe those rumours.

Suddenly out of nowhere the fire alarm went off, the rain outside was getting heavier than before, I remembered from those rumours that the fire alarm would go off at 7pm. I looked at my watch and it was 7pm! We contacted each other to make our way back to the hall in five minutes. Charlotte and Max did not return. We tried to get hold of them but the connection was very poor. Charlotte was running screaming towards us with Max behind her. 'We … we saw a strange figure walking on the school grounds!' As those words shivered out of Charlotte's mouth, all the lights in the school switched off. We all panicked but realised that we had to get our acts together …

Stefania Zeoli
St Michael's Catholic High School, Watford

Ghost

'Mum can I go and look round the house now?'

'Well OK, since I've nearly finished unpacking.'

Ruby then disappeared upstairs while her mother, Jodie, was fussing around putting plates away in the cupboard. It seemed to Jodie that there was endless boxes to go through. She gradually got through each and everyone. With a sigh she flopped on the sofa. Meanwhile Ruby had found her bedroom which was already the colour of a strawberry-pink.

The room suddenly went cold as she could see her own breath. She didn't think much of it for Jodie was calling her down for tea.

Jodie lay in bed reading when a strange wind blew against the curtains and the power went out. Everything was eerie - she heard Ruby's shouts, *one of her nightmares again,* she thought. She slowly got up and went to see Ruby. But she was fast asleep.

Morning came. Ruby stirred her cornflakes in silence. 'What's the matter?' asked Jodie.

'I had a strange dream last night that a girl called Lisa was killed in my bedroom.'

'Well it was just a nightmare so you don't have to worry.'

Ruby went upstairs to her room. She froze in shock! 'Lisa' was written all over the walls in deep red letters. She scrambled downstairs to tell Jodie in a shaken voice what had happened. She grabbed her schoolbag and rushed out of the door while Jodie was left to find out what was going on. She asked the neighbours, where they told her that a girl got killed by her father. Too scared to stay in the house another night, she packed the things she needed and went to get Ruby from school.

That night they stayed at a friend's house, as Jodie thought, would she ever go back to the house because of what had happened?

Sarah Loughran (15)
St Michael's Catholic High School, Watford

A Day In The Life Of Thierry Henry

I woke up and got out of bed. I had a long day ahead, as I was being interviewed by ITV, asking me about my new contract for Arsenal and how I thought the Champions League Final went. I put on my best suit and ate some breakfast. I then went to my garage and got into my Mercedes.

As I pulled into the car park, I saw Arsene Wenger walking into the ITV station. I called to him and we walked to the interview room together. He told me he had been invited as well, and would help me answer the questions. The cameras flashed as soon as I stepped in. We sat down and the interview began.

I was asked the same questions for the whole interview. The reporters found it amusing that when asked about the Champions League Final I said that the referee should have worn a Barcelona shirt, and the Arsenal players should learn to dive. I was also given a round of applause when I said I would stay at Arsenal till the end of my career. Overall I found it an enjoyable experience. Arsene and I went through Arsenal's season with the reporters, explaining how hard it was for us to qualify for the Champions League in the coming season.

After the interview we went to get a coffee Arsene asked me why I wanted to stay at Arsenal? All I said was, 'Arsenal is my home.'

Liam Maguire (11)
St Michael's Catholic High School, Watford

The Competitive Life Of Beth Tweedle

Illuminscent lights shimmering above me lit the whole gymnasium up. The sequins on my leotard glistening like the tropical ocean in the sun.

My heart pounds nervously, rubbing my hands in the moist chalk. Fumbling clumsily with my hand grips the commentator announced my name. I step up to a dulcet applause and make my acknowledgement to the judges, knowing full well that the next few minutes could change my life ...

I remember when it began, three years old experiencing the exhilarating feel of a gymnasium. Right from the start I knew this is where I belonged, people always commented on how I was a natural gymnast, believing it to be an innate ability. Before long gymnastics was my life; my coaches had a master plan for my future. I soon progressed to competitions where the feel for gold medals urged us forward. My need to compete grew like an addiction and the lure of winning was the drug.

For years my body endured great pain but mentally I grew stronger knowing that I was aiming towards my most passionate ambition to be British number one.

My dynamic dismount gave a solid finish. My flawless routine left the judges smiling. The audience were standing! Heading back I gingerly await response. Have I done enough?

A prolonged pause the scores are called; it's all a dream. Looking down on myself there I'm standing on centre podium staring into a gold disc hung around my neck.

I am the British Number One!

Kalisha Ketchen (11)
St Michael's Catholic High School, Watford

A New Person

I woke up and felt different. My skin was paler, my hair was darker and I wasn't who I used to be. I started to panic and raced to the full length mirror to see what was wrong!

I Kayleigh Stammer, the most popular girl in my year, two weeks ago was my birthday and I got a special wishing dust from my brother. I didn't know what to wish for until last night. I wished that I could be the most popular girl in the school - here I am a Kayleigh.

Yesterday I was putting on make-up and spent ages on my hair, not only did I just look like Kayleigh, I also acted like her as well. Once I got to school people chatted to me and so did all the nice-looking boys. I was hanging around with Kayleigh's friends.

Luckily the real Kayleigh was off school today, but no one knew that. Everyone thought that I was the one off school today. After a while I started to realise that my friends are actually fun and that Kayleigh and her friends just stand around chatting and flirting. I felt like I was ditching my friends for popularity.

I had a five-pack of wishing dust, so I used another one and wished that I could turn back to the real me. This morning I felt like myself and got on with my life. I finally realised that good friends mean more to me than popularity.

Lucy Dunne (12)
St Michael's Catholic High School, Watford

Care Falls

It was a cold night, the asylum was as chilling as ever, the pale red tile paved the walls and ceiling, and steel doors lined it. I opened one of the steel doors and behind it was a tube, full of liquid and several holes in the walls. There was a skeletal foot protruding from one but it was too hard to pull out. I continued down the hallway where I spotted a lift. I entered it and pressed the up button. I arrived on the third floor, which was one large room.

Inside this room there were several X-ray pictures and an operating table. I examined some of the X-rays. They had pictures of people with nails, tridents, birds in their stomachs, and an animal with a weird human-like resemblance. I stuffed them into my rucksack and stepped back into the rusty old lift. It rumbled down like a bumpy motorbike, fast and unsafe. I arrived on the first floor where there was no light. It was almost pitch-black but I could see broken down prison cells and cages with the occasional furnace. I heard the zip of a chainsaw. It seemed like an earthquake in the silent environment and within a few seconds something came at me, chainsaw ripping into my flesh. There seemed like no escape.

I called upon all my strength to remove the being and charged towards the lift. The creature followed me but it was too late. It was crushed in the lift and I took him and the chainsaw to forensics. It's a hard life being an android.

Nick Scannell (13)
St Michael's Catholic High School, Watford

The Race Of Her Life

'*The clock ticked away, only seconds to go before the starter pistol and the most important race of her life*'. The race was 1500 metres across country. He watched her from the crowd, dreading the thought of the whole event. His name was Ashley. He's never liked her. An evil smirk was on his face. She just knew that she wouldn't make it to the finish line. *Bang!* She was off!

She approached the 400 metre mark when somebody racing close by to her tripped over a big brown log. From the side of the flags she could see Ashley's face looking eager for her to trip up too.

As the race went on three other runners dropped out, so it left just her and another six runners. As the runners reached the last 600 metres to go, Ashley quickly ran in front of her and the other runners, hoping to put them off. Thankfully he didn't put her off, but she couldn't tell if he had put anyone else off, because they were all behind. She was in the lead. First.

Too scared to look back just in case he was still there and tried to put her off again or trip her up.

The last 400 metre mark was coming up when something happened. She fell to the ground. Not knowing what had just happened and what made her fall, she quickly got back onto her feet again and saw the leader in front of her. She wasn't first anymore. She started quickening her pace to catch up to the leader. She saw Ashley again up ahead. She saw him pull something that looked like string and then she saw the leader fall to the ground.

She was very scared what Ashley might do now. She saw the finish line when she passed the runner on the ground and she started to sprint. She passed the finish line and then saw Ashley again with two policemen standing on either side of him. They had stopped him before he could do anything else. She couldn't believe she had won.

Carl Giacone (13)
St Michael's Catholic High School, Watford

My Haunted Vacation

It was a lovely summer's day, we were all outside in the garden with the small blow-up swimming pool and with the lovely burger and sausage smell from the barbecue. We were all excited because we were going on vacation the next day, we were going to this cabin in the middle of No Man's Wood. We go there every year, we have lots of fun there but this year we decided to go to a different spot, up where all the mountains are looking down on top of the forest. Well we all went to bed at 10 o'clock waiting with excitement for morning to come. The next day.

'Come on, come on, wake up sleepyheads,' my mum said loudly. 'Shannon, get up and wake up Sophie and Jemma. Ashley and Jade are already downstairs waiting for you,' Mum loudly shouted again.

'OK don't worry, I'm up and I'll get those two up now, OK?' I replied nicely.

'OK well get a move on please,' she replied.

'Come on Sophie, come on Jemma, time to get up now, we're going to the forest. Ashley's already downstairs, so we need to hurry up OK?' I quietly said.

'OK then,' Sophie and Jemma replied at the same time.

I got dressed in five minutes with excitement, while Sophie and Jemma had a wash then I helped them get dressed, and before we knew it we were on the road.

It took us three hours to get there, we were playing 'I Spy', we were singing songs and everything was well. We got there at 11.30, the cabin looked all horrible and disgusting, suddenly we weren't excited anymore. When we were bringing all the stuff of ours inside the cabin there was a swinging bench outside the door which was swinging all by itself, we were all a bit freaked out because there was absolutely no sign of any wind.

When we'd put all our stuff down in the rooms we went out to play by the lake with the frisbee we had, when Jemma and Sophie said that they could feel something touching them on the back, but no one was behind them, we all started to get freaked out, even my mum did, but she didn't show it. We all just wanted to go home. So we all started to pack our bags when a bad storm hit us so we couldn't leave.

When the storm blew over we started packing again and finally we all got our stuff together, we rang a taxi to go home, so when we got home we told the rest of the family and they didn't believe us ...

Shannon Santry (12)
St Michael's Catholic High School, Watford

Welcome To Chaos

The clock struck midnight and the neighbourhood was silent. It was the perfect time and place for a raider to snag a priceless artefact. A man dressed in black had just broken into the Museum of Ancient History, home to some of the most valuable pieces in the world. He avoided the security system with the agility and stealth of a cat, and stole 'The Key' and fled to his home.

He then placed it in his collection of stolen treasures. The key had a text on it, but it was in a mysterious language. The raider was anxious to find out what the text meant. He did some research and found the translations.

It was a spell and as he read out loud, a wicked-looking mist suddenly appeared and surrounded the raider. When the mist finally disappeared, the man looked different, he looked like ... he had *wings!* His face became sinister and his eyes were glowing red. He grew scales all over his body just like the red dragon. He had become some sort of demon!

The spell on the key was apparently a transformation spell, it granted the man supernatural powers and took control of his mind. The new demon demolished his home and ascended into the sky with extreme speed. He arrived at the Pacific Ocean in one day. He pointed the key right to the ocean, then a red beam from the key went through the water. The Earth shook with colossal force and a menacing door rose from the depths.

The key flew from the demon's hands and into the keyhole hidden in the demonic portal. The door slowly opened and screams filled the air. A great figure emerged from the portal ... the Earth became Hell.

Richie Soertsz (13)
St Michael's Catholic High School, Watford

A Day In The Life Of A Tree

Awoken. Awoken by a scream. A high-pitched scream followed by pools of laughter. *Smash, smash* again and again. Glass scatters across the pavement. A young girl walks by holding her shoes, her poor achy feet misses a splinter of glass by centimetres. Every weekend is the same. Screams and smashes followed by drunken brawls. I can't wait for the week to begin.

Ah the week has just begun. I stand here swaying in the wind, quietly thinking of a poem.

'So many people I saw today,
Busily on their way,
A man in a top hat
A child with a cap
A woman stopping to have a chat
And a tourist with an upside-down map
How I love to be a tree
I love to see the world go by,
It makes me as happy as can be!'

I like to recite my poems. It helps me block out all the noise of the cars and busy towns nearby. It helps me forget all the bad times with people screaming in pure terror, car brakes screeching and innocent bystanders gasping. Don't get me wrong I have some great times with squirrels and seeing people smiling. One very embarrassing thing is when a dog decided to urinate on me. Charming!

So now you know that being a tree isn't so easy. Like most things it has its ups and downs. Just remember next time you see a tree, smile, it really does make its day!

Kathleen Leahy (13)
St Michael's Catholic High School, Watford

Killer Ghost!

It all came so fast the day I had to move. I didn't want to. We arrived at the house it was a big tower-like building with stained glass windows. I didn't like the look of it.

I pushed the door, its loud creak was piercing, as I walked up the narrow, winding stairs. I felt something brush past me. I turned round but no one was there, so I carried on walking. I eventually came to my room number 106, the door was already open (which was strange) in the corner was a four-poster bed and two chests of drawers. I set out my clothes, make-up posters and CDs but this time I heard someone say, 'Get out otherwise something bad will happen to you and your family.' 'What's that?' I screamed and ran downstairs.

Mum said, 'What's wrong hunny?'

'There's someone in my room, I heard them say we have to go otherwise something bad will happen.'

'It's probably your imagination, it does run wild sometimes!'

We sat down for dinner but I was so paranoid I couldn't eat, so I went up to bed. That's when I saw her there, lying on my bed, with an axe in her hand. I couldn't move. She shot up like a bullet. I jumped. She turned her head, she had blonde hair and her clothes were long but tattered. 'I thought I told you to go,' she said.

'This is our house now, we live here, you go,' I shouted.

With that she raised the axe and chased after me. I was stuck out on a balcony, she raised her axe again but missed. Mum came running in, she'd seen it all from her balcony, she scooped me up and threw me in the car. Me, Mum and Dad drove off, we didn't have time to get our stuff! I saw her standing on the balcony looking at me. I will never forget that night. *Ever!*

Kayleigh Fryer (13)
St Michael's Catholic High School, Watford

Ghost Story

One day a girl called Alex was walking to school. She tripped over a coin and the coin had writing on the side, it said, 'Whoever takes this coin will be cursed'. But she did not believe in that stuff so she took it and then carried on walking, then the sky went dark. Suddenly a lady came from the sky, she had a pale white face and a black dress on. She looked so scary, then the lady said as she was descending down, 'You took my coin now you shall pay!'

Alex did not know if it was a joke or not and she decided that it wasn't a joke, so she ran as fast as ever.

Finally she came to the end of Woodherst Avenue and her school was now in sight. When she got to school people were asking her why she was running. She did not know why they couldn't see the ghost. She ran in the school hall, the ghost got her cornered then the bell went. It gave her a chance to leave and so she took it.

She thought, *where would a ghost not go?* And she went there and stayed there till dark, then she thought, *I have to face her* and she went and said, 'What do you want from me?'

Then the ghost said, 'Your soul,' and so it took it and possibly it would take yours too, so watch out, it might be everywhere or anywhere …

Samantha May (12)
St Michael's Catholic High School, Watford

A Strange Day

I know I've seen her face before. I must find her in this photo album, that's her! Clarina Arvarchi. I knew it! I used to go round her house but now we are in secondary school I don't know her anymore.

I saw Alicia today she's still Miss Popular. I can't believe I used to play with her. I don't care. I don't need her anymore.

I think that was the worst night in my life. I must have slept awkwardly. This isn't my room, that's not my face, what has happened to my nails? Oh my goodness I'm Clarina.

Last night I found it hard to sleep. I was thinking about Alicia and now I'm awake in her body and her room.

I'm going to go to school as Clarina, I wonder what it's like to be her. She always hangs around with, well I don't know, but I soon will.

Alicia has such a strange life, I went to school as her today and I was told by her friends that unless I was mean to people I was out. Now I know why she's a bully.

I can't understand why Clarina lets herself be bullied, it's awful. I've got to find a way to help her.

Well today was a day like no other and we switched back bodies only a moment ago and we have decided to be best friends again. We couldn't be happier, although we still don't know how our bodies were switched.

Helen Keith (13)
St Michael's Catholic High School, Watford

Betrayed

Me and my best friend Jenny have been so close since nursery. We have always done everything together; I really don't know where I would be without her. We are both seventeen and in college. I can't wait until we go to university together.

Fridays are always the best day of the week. College is on from eleven to two and then there's nothing to do. Normally Jenny and me would get some chips and then go to hers or mine for the night. Today after college, we went to the fish and chip shop, got some chips then drove to her house. We just quickly ran into her house so she could get her sleeping stuff. Then we just drove back to mine.

Once we'd arrived we went straight up to my room. Jenny gave me a huge grin. 'What's up Jen?' I asked.

She sat me down on the bed, 'Well tonight's the biggest party of the year! We have to go!'

I smiled and nodded my head vigorously. 'OK, we'll have to sneak out though.' We both shrugged it off and began to giggle.

At nine o'clock after watching my parents' boring TV shows, we all went upstairs. My parents went to bed but me and Jenny got all dolled up for the party and snuck out.

Within half an hour of the party, boys were flirting with me, even though they knew I had a boyfriend. So I told them to go and talk to Jenny because she is single, but they refused.

Once Jamie came over to talk to me about school, Jenny dragged me out into the middle of the woods. It was dark and she was drunk. I was afraid. She began to shout abuse at me, because she fancied Jamie, and when I tried to defend myself, Jenny just banged my head against a tree trunk, until I was dead. And yet, my biggest regret wasn't sneaking out, but not letting my parents know that I love them so much.

Sabrina Cesaratto (13)
St Michael's Catholic High School, Watford

The Minotaur

The sirens were flashing and making noise as the Minotaur raised havoc on the city. It ran, roaring, destroying anything in its path. How it got here, no one knows.

On the 23rd October 2006 Tim Roberts reportedly sighted a half man half bull in a New York sewer at 14.20. Half an hour later the beast was on a rampage.

At 15.00 the SWAT team were on 23rd Street in Brooklyn chasing the beast. It got shot a couple of times but kept on running. It smashed cars, powerlines and people. Soon after 15.00 martial law was declared throughout all of New York and some other places just outside New York. The beast had left Brooklyn. It was shot down and killed by 15.15. It had killed two people and injured twenty, but police asked, 'Where did it come from?' The monster was seven feet tall, light brown and human up to the waist. Martial law was declared because police didn't know how many Minotaurs there were, and it was moving quickly.

It was an eventful day for Brooklyn, and the martial law was called off at 17.00. The people acted well and there were almost no riots. It is a possibility that there is another Minotaur somewhere on Earth, but no one knows.

James Cottee (13)
St Michael's Catholic High School, Watford

The Rumour About Couper Hill

Everyone in our area knew the rumours surrounding the Couper Hills. We'd grown up in the area and had spent most of our childhood playing there with my friend Laura. Laura and I had been friends since we were first born, and that is how I intend it to stay.

One day Laura and I wanted to find out if these rumours were true. So that night we decided to go down to the woods at midnight to see if there were really ghosts wandering the woods.

That night Laura slept round, at about 11.45pm we crept out of the house and ran down to the woods. We waited and waited. Then suddenly, there was a loud groaning noise, Laura and I were petrified. What could it have been? There it was again. Laura and I turned round and there it was. A ghost. Standing right in front of us, the ghost looked like a poltergeist; he hovered around us with chains on his legs and arms with the body of a dead girl hanging in his arms. Laura and I ran home as fast as we could.

The next morning, as soon as it was breakfast time, Laura and I came bursting through the doors.

'Mum, Mum!' I shouted.

'What?' she cried, thinking we had hurt ourselves.

'Last night we went down to the woods and we saw a dead man walking round with a body in his arms, the rumours are true.'

'I'm sure you did girls, but if you don't mind, I have some important things to do.' Mum said.

'But we did Mum, it is not a lie,' I anticipated her reaction.

'You girls do have some imagination,' she said, doubtfully.

Well at least we know that the rumours of Couper Hill do exist, and that's a fact.

Chloé Couper (13)
St Michael's Catholic High School, Watford

Untitled

I sit here knowing I am a week away from my SATs. I have been revising for the last month, yet I am still nervous about it all, and I wonder how well I will do.

When I get home I will have my dinner, revise and then go to football training with my team. So I started to train and I was playing my usual game, but then halfway through I kept on hearing these voices, but there was no one around me. It was like it was a ghost but he wasn't haunting, he was helping me.

I returned home later that evening and Dad said, 'Was it good?'

I replied, 'Yes, but I kept on hearing a voice, it was a ghost helping me.'

This week I had got my SATs, I was nervous but excited because I knew I could do well. First I had got my maths exam so I went into the hall, and halfway through I started to hear this voice, it was the ghost and he was helping me again. At first I thought he was going to be horrible, but he helped me and somehow we became close. I am pleased with myself because I think I have done well, all thanks to the ghost.

Ashley Toomey (12)
St Michael's Catholic High School, Watford

Walking With Ghosts

It was a cold night and Louise Stafford was spending her first night in her new house. It was a fairly small house on the edge of London with a large garden and two rooms. She was living on her own because her fiancé Tom Olmedilla, had recently died in a car accident.

On her first day in the house she kept hearing a strange noise in the attic; she ignored it for the night and called a pest control officer in the morning. When he came and checked it out he said he could see nothing but he would lay traps down just in case there was something. After a few weeks this noise carried on so Louise went up to check it out herself.

Nothing was there so she just thought she was being paranoid, in the night she had a dream about Tom, this was normal, but strangely her dream seemed really real. She could smell him on her bed, she could hear his voice, she could feel him next to her. After a while she kept on finding little things around her house that would mean nothing to anyone else, but meant quite a lot to her. Like all her socks were folded, and the lights were always off. There was only one person who she knew that did this. Tom. After a while she started to suspect that something was going on. She had a lady in to communicate with the dead. The lady found that Tom had been following her and leaving signs to show he was there, she managed to speak to him and told him that Louise was missing him and loved him very much.

This must have been one of the strangest couples alive, but Louise and Tom managed to live together and stay very happy and stay very much in love. They were still a very happy couple, even though they couldn't see or touch each other when they were awake.

Lily Goff (13)
St Michael's Catholic High School, Watford

Three Pints Of Blood

In the summer of 2003 James Gibson was found guilty of manslaughter, his sentence was a life sentence. He was a fresh-faced 21-year-old that had everything going for him; he had lots of friends and a loving family. It was on one night that changed everything.

He had rented out a film from the local video store and it was called 'Dracula 2000' It seemed pretty harmless, until he started to like the film a lot, he watched it a lot. A few weeks after this was still going on, he had taken the film back though and bought a copy, the film was about vampires, pretty strange but a good film.

Months passed and this film was watched night on end, he began to revise the words and became less social, he sometimes never left the house for days on end. In these times he never left the house, the main character of the film would speak to him, tell him to do things like harm other people, he began to go into a scary, trance, but was still in the real world.

When he left the house one morning he was twitching and acted very nervous walking along the streets in the local shopping high street, he was holding a knife in his hand, and he was on the way to his best friend's house.

James knocked at the door of Joseph Jackson's house, he gripped the knife tightly in his pocket and waited for his best friend to open the door, as the door creaked open, James began to sweat, he walked into his best friend's house and before he knew it, he had plunged the knife into Joseph. Moments later in James' head the main character of the film said for him to do terrible things to the body that are too gruesome to say, but when Joseph's body was found, he had half his head chopped off and had approximately three pints of blood missing.

'It was the worst feeling I've ever had, I had to identify my son's body,' said Sarah Jackson, the mother of James Gibson's best friend. This is what a film could do to you.

Jemma Coyle (13)
St Michael's Catholic High School, Watford

A Day In The Life Of John Terry

It was Sunday and I was getting ready for the football match and in the changing room, José told us who were the subs, and who we were marking.

Today's opposition is Manchester Utd., I am marking Wayne Rooney, and we as a team, had an excellent start. William Gallas scored with a header after 11 mins of the match. Sir Alex Ferguson was not a happy manager. Wayne Rooney had a bad accident and broke a bone in his foot, and so we score two more goals to win 3-0 and won the Premiership. What celebrations followed, both on the pitch with our supporters and afterwards with our friends and family, it was one of the best days of my life.

I got a bad cut on my leg, but my medical team said I would be OK for the World Cup in Germany in June when I expect England to bring home the Cup. 2006 promises to be a very exciting year winning the Premiership, possibly the World Cup, and later this year, I hope to become the proud father of twins.

Christopher Low (13)
St Michael's Catholic High School, Watford

White Horse

In the summer holidays I went to stay with my grandma because my mum and dad had to go away for two weeks. I was so bored the first week there, all my gran talked to me about was her childhood, but it sounded fun, so I kept dreaming of being her age in her time, it would have been the best ever.

On the Saturday of the first week I was so bored, so I just went to the bottom of the field and there was this beautiful white horse it was just like the one my grandma had described to me. This horse was so beautiful I couldn't take my eyes off it, I went inside to get some carrots and apples for the horse. I looked after this horse all week, it let me ride on it, feed it, groom it, anything I wanted. I loved this horse so much by the end of the week. I had to go that night, I was crying, because I knew I could not take the horse with me. I was saying goodbye to Grandma and I almost forgot to say goodbye to the beautiful horse that I named Beauty, so I asked, 'Can I go and say bye to my horse?'

My grandma said, 'What horse? I have no horse anymore. I had one when I was twelve but it died, it was so beautiful I named it Beauty, it was white and so calm. I loved it so much and when it went I cried so much I still feel the tears now.'

'But I have been with your horse all week ...'

Hannah Gornicki (12)
St Michael's Catholic High School, Watford

The Psychiatrist From Hell

I slowly opened the door not knowing what sort of person I would be meeting. A small old woman was standing at the door to greet me; she had an annoying crooked smile with large gleaming white teeth. She directed me to a chair in the corner of the room. She sat down in front of me and started to ask some unusual questions about my social life.

The only reason that I was there was because my friends bullied me about my ears, as they stick out a bit. But my mum forced me to go.

The temperature of the room was unbearable, but the little woman, known as Claire, said that workers were fixing the air conditioning. I kept disagreeing with the pointless questions she was asking me, but she wouldn't give in.

Most of the things she said went unheard due to the terrible screeching of the drills next door.

She would constantly ask my mum and I if we wanted some peanuts or a drink of water, but I was quick to pass.

The room was small, dark and it smelt like something had died and decomposed in the floorboards. I was so desperate to get out. I kept asking if I could go to the toilet and thankfully I was allowed.

But I will never know how long it took them to realise that I had gone past the toilets and straight home.

Sam Barratt (13)
St Michael's Catholic High School, Watford

The Assassination

It was a warm Sunday morning. But unusually there was a crowd of people outside number 12 Downing Street. There was a good reason for this however. The president was in there with the prime minister. As they walked out a AK7 pistol with a silencer was drawn and without pausing he shot. It was pandemonium as the president fell bleeding to the ground. He was already dead.

'It has been two weeks and we haven't found anything,' he exclaimed.
'We better call him.'
William Goldsmith was an elderly man. You wouldn't have guessed from looking at him that this elderly man had caught some of the most dangerous criminals in the world.
'The bullet was short range so I want everyone within 20 feet of the president put in a room.'
'Why?'
'Because when people are in a room they talk.'
The collection of people in that room was amazing. From the prime minister looking rather nervous to bodyguards looking scary. 'I have a confession,' the prime minister said, 'I think this is a waste of time.'
'Hear, hear,' the rest of them exclaimed.
Will Goldsmith then realised who it was, it was so obvious he had the motive and he had the tools.
'It was you, wasn't it?' he exclaimed.
'No.' He was still nervous. 'OK I did but he was ruining my career, so I got rid of him.'
'I'm afraid you're under arrest, prime minister!'

James Knight (13)
St Michael's Catholic High School, Watford

Dennis Bergkamp

It was Thursday and I was getting ready for a photoshoot for Arsenal 2006 calendar. Then I was going to go and pick up my new car, it's a Carrera GT. I got the car and went to the match against Blackburn Rovers, I was in the changing room and getting ready for kick-off.

We all got ready to go out but I was always going to be on the bench. I am getting a bit older now, and need not to be doing a lot of football and getting an injury.

We were playing our best, and my close friend, Henry, got a great goal. We had won and we were all on a high, we went back into the changing room and celebrated. It was 6 o'clock and we were ready to party. I went out with the boys until 10 o'clock. I then went to see the family at home. We had another match tomorrow against Man U, it was the FA Cup semi final and we needed to win.

Time to go to bed that's all in the life of Dennis Bergkamp; but in the middle of the night I got a phone call saying that Henry had broken his foot, I went to see him and he said he would be fine, I went back home to bed, but as you can see it's not all fun when you're a footballer!

Ben Simmons (13)
St Michael's Catholic High School, Watford

A Day In The Life Of Andy Pipkin

It was an ordinary day like any other day; that's what I thought.

On Saturday I woke up at 10am to watch the new movie that I bought yesterday. I was looking forward to watching the new movie because it was 'Little Britain' and I love watching 'Little Britain'.

I started to watch it and it was so funny to watch and I could hardly breathe because of it. Then I started to feel very tired because I'd had a very late night last night, so in about five minutes I fell asleep.

When I woke up, the movie had already finished. I wasn't worried about that because I was feeling very strange. I knew there was something wrong. I looked at myself and saw a wheelchair which I was sitting in. I could see myself in the TV and I had turned into Andy Pipkin.

I said, 'I don't like it, I wanna be myself.' I was so shocked, I didn't know what to do. After I'd calmed down, I noticed it was hot outside. I thought to myself, *I wanna go swimming,* so I did. I was going to enjoy myself being Andy Pipkin.

I've had great fun today, but sooner or later I'll have to turn back to normal. Suddenly a ghost came out from the wall and said, 'You have until midnight before you turn back to normal.' It was now 8pm.

I had some dinner and then went to bed hoping that all would be back to normal in the morning.

In the morning I woke up at 9.30am and I was back to normal again. *What will happen next?*

Sean Smith (13)
St Michael's Catholic High School, Watford

A Day In The Life ...

Live broadcast from Andy Townsend on the Champions League Final.

'The biggest game of the season yet, the Club's version of the World Cup, the Champions League Final between Arsenal the underdogs and Barcelona the favourites.

The game starts. Eto'o slickly passes it to Ronaldinho, he bamboozles one defender and beautifully delivers it to Messi who runs along the wing like Roadrunner. He is halted quickly as Senderos tramples over him like a train. Ronaldinho swings the ball in so easily and majestically and Xavi rises up like a tidal wave and ploughs the ball into the net. First blood to Barcelona! Barcelona controls the game after that with Deco hitting the post, and Eto'o is forced over as Lehmann fights hard not to concede another. Until Ljunberg loses the ball, and Eto'o sprints through like Morris Greene and pelts the ball like a cannonball into the net. 2-0!

Half-Time

Arsenal come out fighting, strong, contesting with and the right mentality to win. Reyes has the ball, runs on like Forest Gump through the defence and lays it back to Hleb running on who taps it into the net. 2-1, Comeback has begun! A mixed game through this period with Arsenal snapping at Barcelona's heels like a raged Jack Russel against a feared Rotweiller. Henry gets the ball outside the area, no one for support, shoots gloriously, it floats through the air and cruises like a ship in the Atlantic to the top corner of the net. 2-2.

Added time nerves spread through the team like bacteria can something become triumphant. Fabregas on the ball one-two with Gilberto runs forward passes to Ljungberg on the left dummies past Marquez and crosses it in. The ball seems to travel in slow motion to Bergkamp, controls it with his shoulder and volleys it into the roof of the net. *Goal!* 3-2.

Arsenal have won the Champions League and are the new kings of Europe.

James Creber (12)
St Michael's Catholic High School, Watford

You Think He'll Be Mad?

Hi I'm Sara Benford. I've always got my own way well normally because you see, the other day I was 45 minutes late home. I was having so much fun I lost track of time.

And now for the first time in my life I'm grounded! Which is really unfair partly because it's my best friend's birthday party tomorrow and I can't go.

Today I'm meant to be going shopping with Sophie for a new outfit for the party.

I'm not allowed to use the phone. I'm not even allowed out of my room. Unless ... I sneak out because Dad won't be back until 6 30pm so he won't know.

Later on ...

OK I'm at the mall. I took Daddy's credit card. So I'm ready to shop till I drop. Where on earth is Sophie? Oh there she is. I hope she's got money to spend, spend, spend!

I just love shopping, or how the French say: J'adore acheter.

I've just bought a really nice black leather mini skirt and some cream sandals. Now I just need a top.

'Sophie look at that top, it's gorgeous.'

'Yeah it's lovely, you should get it!'

'I am.'

'Oh where's Daddy's credit card?'

'What! You've lost it!'

'Let's go look for it.'

Back at home.

'Dad, I'm really, really sorry but I lost your credit card,' I said crying my eyes out.

'Go to your room and I don't want to see you again until tomorrow.' He said, sounding so ashamed and disappointed in me.

Now I feel ashamed ...

Kayleigh O'Brien (12)
St Michael's Catholic High School, Watford

The Mysterious Moment

One summer day at the beach, Mum had gone to get us an ice cream when suddenly the sun went down, it must have only been 2 o'clock.

Mum had been gone for ages so we went looking for her. We found this amazing cave so we went exploring. I lost track of my friends. There were footsteps behind me, panicking to escape I squeezed through a gap. I jumped on a boat going out to sea, it was really rough, I must have been knocked out, but when I woke up I was just grounding on to an island.

On this island there was lots of signs and arrows which I felt compelled to follow. I came across an ancient burial ground where one of the graves had been disturbed by someone who had been looking for buried treasure.

The burial ground needed to be restored to its previous state. I toiled away day and night until I finally collapsed in a state of exhaustion. The job was done and the sound of footsteps had stopped.

I walked down towards the beach wondering how I was going to get home. Then I heard a whirling noise, it was getting nearer and louder it sounded like a helicopter.

The next thing I remember was my friends telling me to hurry up as my ice cream was melting.

They asked me where had I been. What was I to say? How could I explain the unexplainable?

April Cope (12)
St Michael's Catholic High School, Watford

The Life Of A Cat

What a night! I was so hungry after the fight I'd had with the other cat down the street, I strolled down the big stairs; as my family got dressed for school. I saw my mum packing their tasty, mouth-watering lunch, I wanted some, I was waving my furry white tail for attention and to move my mum to the silver sparkling bowl for my food, I was growling and growling then my mum saw me, 'Hang on a bit Saffy,' then my food came. Lovely Whiskas, my favourite. I launched my face at the tuna food, I was full, my tummy was feeling like it was going to burst!

Satisfied, I headed for the conservatory where it was warm and cosy and cuddled up on my favourite cushion for a nap.

A couple of hours later I could hear the birds in the garden, so I decided to go out and have a game with them. Very quietly I crept out of the window and sneaking along the wall of the house, I tiptoed towards a finch who was looking for wiggly worms.

Pounce! I jumped forward, shocking him. Inside I was laughing to myself, he flew up into the air and I chased after him. This is how I spent my afternoon.

Feeling tired I decided to go back in the house. Suddenly I felt like a drink, nice cold milk was just what I needed after a hard day out. After my drink I curled up on my mum's bed where it was nice and cool.

When I woke up it was dark, 'Hooray!' it was time to go out and meet my mates, for a night of hunting.

Josh Austin (12)
St Michael's Catholic High School, Watford

Whistles In The Wind

Why is it that younger children are frightened when the wind whistles? Or why when you're alone outside in the dark and the trees are blowing, and the wind whistles making you look behind you, just to check? Well I'll tell you:

Long, long ago a woman lived in a little cottage, she was not any woman, she was a witch, nobody knew except the children. They would walk a longer way just to avoid her house, because they knew if they got too close she would whistle. Her whistle was irresistible, if a child heard it they would be in a trance and walk straight into her house where she would cast spells and take their young spirits to keep herself young, then she would burn their bodies. She was a cruel woman, and spared not one thought for the parents and families of these dear children.

One night she cast a spell to make a huge wind go all over the town, then she began to whistle, the wind swept her whistle through the town but she accidentally knocked over her lantern, the house was quickly full of leaping flames. She carried on whistling, the children had climbed out of their beds and were walking through the town, they walked into the climbing flames with the witch. The next day all that the parents had left of their precious children was the ashes of their bodies entwined with the witch's.

That's why the wind whistles, because the wind is still under the witch's spell, and always will be, so that's why children are scared of the whistles in the wind, they can feel her calling them.

Sophie Hendricks (13)
St Michael's Catholic High School, Watford

It

'Oi! Come here!' The tall and beefy Year 11 shouted at my worried-looking face. I tried to act hard and shouted back.

'What do you want?' I spat at him.

'I want what you stole from my locker you thief!'

I backed away at his foul-smelling breath and rotten teeth.

'I ain't stolen anything from you!' Before I knew it he had kicked me down onto the grey concrete floor and grabbed my bag, tipping it upside-down spilling my books, pens and pencils on the floor.

'What have you done with it? I want it back you lousy thief!'

He chucked my bag back at me as, I timidly said, 'I don't know what you're talking about, I haven't been into anyone else's locker but mine!' I lied. I knew exactly what he was talking about, I didn't steal it though, it was in the changing rooms, left out amongst the uniform of Year 11s, I couldn't resist but take a look at it. It was then that I ran out of the changing rooms, as I could hear them coming in from PE, taking it with me. I never meant to steal it.

'Well then who was it?'

I had a plan, I would give them a name of someone else in my year so I could get away and return it without anyone knowing. 'D-D-Daniel Carter.' I stuttered the name out of my mouth knowing it was a cowardly thing to do. The Year 11 punched me in the face, then walked away leaving me cowering on the floor. I grabbed my bag and books and hurried off to the changing rooms hoping he'd think it had been there all along.

Danielle Sapwell (13)
St Michael's Catholic High School, Watford

Short Story

On a dark, dark day and a dark, dark night, four little children were given a fright. One was big, one was tall, one was fat and one was small. They saw a dark shadow in the trees, it was so scary they fell to their knees. One by one they started to crawl around the outside swimming pool.

One fell in and bumped his head, the small one cried, 'I think he's dead!'

'Course I'm not you stupid fool, don't you be so flipping cruel.'

The fat one pulled him from the water because he thought he really oughta.

The shadow moved with agile grace, a twisted look upon its face. The children ran towards the house, it followed them the evil louse.

The big one said, 'We need a plan to rid us of this scary man.'

'Whose house is this that we are in?'

'Is the shadow out there or here within?'

The fat one said, 'I just don't care I'm cold and wet and so is my hair.'

The door flew open and they saw its face, at once they knew they'd lost the race.

And so it ends my tale of woe, what became of them we'll never know.

Ashley Wright (13)
St Michael's Catholic High School, Watford

The Golden Eagle

There once lived a town, a small town hanging off the edge of the world. And in that town was a large mountain which they called Demon Edge because anyone that ever went up there either came back terribly injured, mental or never even came back at all! At the top of the hill stood a golden eagle which everyone saw as the sunset.

One day hardworking, average man, David Johnson turned up just in time for work for his company, Globadex, a company used to doing highly dangerous and exciting things. Although David did none of that he just worked in the office. However his boss Mr Cleves said that he would have to accompany the team on a new challenge in exploring Demon Edge!

So they set off on their journey up the hill, there was David, Mr Cleves and two apprentices, Mike and Declan. They got into the cave and could hear noises, suddenly a bit of the ground fell through, Mike and Declan had suddenly vanished into the open space and fallen to their deaths, so it was left to David and Mr Cleves to try and find a way out of the dark, creepy, cold cave.

They came across an enormous monster, a cross between a dragon and an elephant. Mr Cleves took a sword and tried to stab the beast but he just swept him aside to his death, then he locked his concentration on David. The monster was just about to knock David out before he was rescued by the golden eagle who carried him above the whole town before landing him safely. All of a sudden people started to gather round David as the eagle flew away onto the top of the cliff just as the sun set.

Calum Ryan
St Michael's Catholic High School, Watford

Spooky

Last winter we moved into our house, it was a very dull and spooky-looking house. It was late by the time we moved our things in. My room was big but very old and creepy. In the corner was a ladder leading to a hatch. I tried to open it but it was stuck. It was getting late so I got ready for bed and settled down with my book.

After a while, I heard scratching noises coming from the attic, I laid very still, listening. Then I heard a loud *bang!* I covered my head with my duvet, shaking. I heard nothing else after that and went to sleep. In the morning I told my dad I thought there was a ghost in the attic. He managed to open the hatch. There was nothing up there but old boxes. He said it was all in my mind. I agreed and nothing else was said.

When I went to bed that night the noises started again. I was scared. I thought this was silly. So I got up and slowly climbed the ladder into the attic. I stood up and looked into the darkness Something suddenly jumped on my head. I screamed really loudly, and Dad came running in and turned the light on. I opened my eyes to find a small cat sitting in front of me. The cat miaowed and we both laughed.

The so-called ghost that I was so scared of turned out to be a cat. We decided to keep her and called her Spooky. And since that night I've slept like a baby.

Tiffany Norman (13)
St Michael's Catholic High School, Watford

A Day In The Life Of A Cat!

I woke up with a start. The front door slammed and coats and bags were thrown on the sofa where I had been sleeping. I could hear my cat bowl being moved. Yay! My owner, Sam, had bought me some crunchies. I purred loudly and ran over to him. He bent down to stroke my long brown fur. I looked out the window, it was dark and windy.

My crunchies tasted lovely! I waited at the door for five minutes hoping someone would let me out. But as usual they were busy. So I started to make scratching noises at the door. Yes! Someone noticed me. 'Alright, alright, I'm coming!' they said. I darted out the door.

There were other cats at the bottom of the garden but they ran away like bullets. They were much older than me. The old lady next door called me over. She said something strange, so I shouted at her. 'I'm not a baby, so why are you talking to me like that?' but she cooed at me even more! How annoying!

I then amused myself by digging up her plants. She tried to run after me. I ran even faster as she had the gardening fork in her left hand.

I loved playing with the dog on the other side of the garden. He seemed to really love cats. He pulled a face at me when I went to leave for dinner. But I told him of course I would be back tomorrow.

Lauren Done (13)
St Michael's Catholic High School, Watford

A Day In The Life Of My Dog - A Morning

I opened my eyes and saw Daisy, the other dog that is in the house where I live. I climbed out of my bed and stretched out to help wake me up. I went through to the kitchen and went towards my food bowl. Jack, my owner, was sitting down eating some type of food. My food and water bowl were empty so I looked up at Jack and barked, until he realised that I wanted him to fill them up. He went over to the cupboard where the food was kept and took out the bag of food. He then picked up the bowl and filled it with water on one side and food on the other, he placed it down by a long wooden thing. I took some of the bigger pieces of food and then I drank almost all of the water.

After I had finished I walked back into the area where my bed is, and looked around to see if I could find Lisa, who would walk me and Daisy. I pushed through the door that went into a long-looking place. I had heard Jack call it a 'hallway'. Lisa was in front of me holding the long red thing she clipped onto me. I knew it was time to go to the place where there was that soft-feeling thing all over the ground. I knew in my mind today would be a good day.

Jack Moore (13)
St Michael's Catholic High School, Watford

Another London Day

I wake up with the beaming winter sun piercing my eyes with its purifying light. I cannot open my eyes for again the winter frost has sealed them together. I can hear the pitter-patter of shoes rushing among the pavement. Stampedes of busy cars in such a rush, but yet sat still in a mile-long traffic jam. Big Ben's chimes echoing into the distance, whilst standing strong and proud in the winter mist. The tips of my fingers are stone cold. I can barely feel them. Oh what I wouldn't do for a second blanket. Although I am luckily still breathing my lungs feel like they have frozen over. It is painful to breathe, but yet I take a deep breath. I smell factory fumes, wasted garbage and an elegant perfume from a sophisticated lady just gone by. There's a sense of a sudden rush, people rushing past as if the world's going to end tomorrow. I open my eyes and yet again I am born to another London day.

A cascade of people in a sudden rush. Men in three-piece linen suits. Elegant ladies dressed to professional perfection. Tourists travelling and sightseeing. Trying to weave their way round London with a little pocket map. Little children clinging onto their mums for dear life, afraid of being swallowed up by the upcoming crowd. Elderly ladies holding onto what little they have left. Upper class businessmen glare down at me with disgust as if I'm a piece of sxxt rather like the one I'm accidentally sat on. I heave my frozen body up and off the ground. My body is still. I glide my fingers through my hair, to attempt at looking half decent. People staring at me as if I'm some sort of nearly extinct species. I straighten myself up. I can barely stand. but that's what you get for not eating for three days.

Here comes the street warden again, I must gather up what little belongings I own and be on my way. I haven't exactly got much to pack, just my duvet and a bottle of water that someone ungratefully threw into the bin the other day, when they could have just as easily passed it to me. But oh well I still got it in the end! I pack them into a plastic bin bag, sling them over my shoulder and start to make my way down Oxford Street.

My feet feel sore and blistered and they are probably as black as the night sky. I cannot pick up my feet; instead I am forced to drag them along the dirty mistreated pavement. I haven't been able to look at my feet for coming up to two years, because I cannot take my shoes off because my feet are continually swollen, and besides I cannot take the risk of my shoes being nicked by the local tramp down the street, for I cannot just go out and buy another pair.

Christine Scott (15)
St Michael's Catholic High School, Watford

A Day In The Life Of A WWII Soldier

June 7th 1944

I cannot describe how I feel. The weight of uncertainty is so heavy I can't take it anymore. We were briefed only five minutes ago. We need to do the job quick. Job? What job? I do not understand why they are talking to us like it's our final moments. We have not been told what to expect. All they have said that we are going to have to be quick on the trigger. But why? Why is it that we need to be like this? I can't see what resistance we are going to face! ...

Seven hours later.

500 men. All going up one beach. That's a lot of people, I thought. But then it hit me. All the hints were there. If I had only paid attention. The Germans have got huge bunkers set up and lots of machine-gun nests placed. We'll be running up a hill to Hell and the only way back is to be killed. Cruel choice.

30 seconds to drop off. Bullets are zipping around all over the place. Bombs going off like there's no tomorrow, but maybe there is no tomorrow for me and my comrades.

10 seconds. I feel so sick and nervous. I don't fear death, it's just that I fear losing my family. But they will be fine, I hope. 4, 3, 2, here we go, no turning back, *bang!*

The door hatch opens with a loud bang. Everyone just falling to the ground in front of me, there's no way through, I'm gonna have to bale over ...

Luke Godfrey (15)
St Michael's Catholic High School, Watford

Everyday Life As A Shark

Eyes rolled back in my head, getting faster, tail thrashing, my five-star lunch has arrived.

Munching down on the blubber of a seal, I swim away in the deep blue.

Digesting the seal, I see a big piece of meat floating in the water, as I get nearer the meat disappears, as I turn away, the meat reappears in front of me. I lurched forward for the meat, one big jump to reach the meat, a hand reached out and touched my nose as I swam away.

As I sensed my family I followed them deeper into the sea. A rope dropped from the boat and picked up my mum as I started thrashing to save her, she said to me to swim away.

I didn't understand why I had to leave my mum knowing I would never see her again. My dad explained to me why we had to leave my mum, it was because of the beings who prey on the women and she didn't want me to die with her.

After two days when I was getting over the fact that I would never see my mum again, my dad and I went to find food with my brothers.

An hour went by when we saw a pod of dolphins gathering a school of fish. We waited and hovered above the sardines when the dolphins gathered them in a whirlpool, my eyes rolled back, in my head, getting faster, tail thrashing, my three-star meal had arrived.

Lynsey Gray (15)
St Michael's Catholic High School, Watford

My Ghost Story

I felt the presence. I knew he was there. I didn't mean to. It wasn't my fault. I only pushed him for my own good. I didn't think it would kill him. Why then? Why me and why him?

It was 1am and I began to close up the pub, the last round had been ordered and the people began to leave except the odd one or two that had to be forced out because of too much alcohol. The weather outside was bitter. I remember it clearly because it stung my face and hands. The sky was jet-black apart from the twinkles from a few stars above. I wrapped up warm in my furry coat, scarf and gloves.

My house was only fifteen minutes away, so I decided to walk rather than cycle. The roads were icy from the rain earlier, the wind was minus five degrees.

The peacefulness of night was exhilarating. All I could hear was the sound of my shoes on the pavement. It would have been a brilliant night to sleep under the stars. I could see the house lights from some of the houses down the street. It was very late for some people to be up. Still I was enjoying the peacefulness of the night rather than worrying about other people. I was coming up to the bridge, I walked over to get to my house and decided to look down at the river below. That night it seemed as though the river was dancing in pairs. It was so amazing the way the river ran so smoothly in the midnight air. I went into my own dreamworld for five minutes and realised I'd better go home and see my boyfriend before he went looking for me.

I turned around to realise there was someone behind me. I didn't know what to do so I carried on walking. He grabbed my arm and pushed me to the side of the bridge wall. Suddenly the river didn't seem to be dancing anymore, the small waves were fighting each other and blackness of the night wasn't peaceful, it was terrifying. He gave me a grin as if to say you know what's going to happen. His hand moved to my leg and I gave a scream. He moved his hand to my mouth and whispered in my ear, 'Do you want to live past tonight? Because if you do I suggest that you be quiet ...'

Rebecca Burt (15)
St Michael's Catholic High School, Watford

Untitled

'I call this room,' Jerome shouted.

Somehow I didn't think so. There was no way was he getting the biggest room. I'm sixteen and I need space plus girls take up more room.

'I didn't think so I need more space than you plus I'm older!' I screamed back at him. He wasn't having any of it. He wanted that room and that was what he thought he was going to get. 'How about we toss a coin for it?' So we did, I called heads and of course I won! Jerome walked out with a face like he had been slapped with a wet fish.

It took six long hours to sort out my room. It looked great. The walls were white. There was a four-poster bed with pink sheets and all accessories were out in the right places. Nothing looked out of place. I sighed in relief. It was now 11.30 and I need to sleep. All the rest of the family were in bed and I was the last up as usual.

I was lying in bed and was just about to fall asleep when I heard this noise coming from the attic. It was like footsteps above my head. The noise started to get louder and louder and even heavier. I pulled the covers over my head and began to play on my mobile. This always seemed to calm me down, but no I couldn't ignore this noise. Then suddenly it stopped. I pulled back the cover slowly and screamed. There was Jerome standing over me.

'Did you hear it? That noise like footsteps?'

I told him to stop being stupid. But I knew exactly what he heard. I wasn't imagining it, there was something going on. My door opened again, I looked up. I froze, I didn't know what to do. Who was he? And what was he doing? ...

Zara Coalwood (15)
St Michael's Catholic High School, Watford

Ghost Story

The year was 1998. The Cross family decided to move from the big high flying city out to the quiet place of the suburbs. They were moving into an old Victorian house that had been there for decades. It was beautiful with great big high ceilings and all the original furniture. He felt like they had something that was a part of history. What they didn't know was that they also got someone who was a part of history too.

The first night they moved in everything was fine until they all went to bed. Sasha, Mr and Mrs Cross' daughter, could hear a rattling in her room, it was getting annoying and she became irritated, so she got up to see what it was. Then Sasha could see her closet door moving as if someone was trying to get out, so she gently opened the door. Her hands were trembling and she had gone as white as a ghost. Suddenly something pushed her and the closet door was slammed shut and locked straight away. But what was it that had put her in there? Then a voice started saying, 'Get out, get out.'

Sasha immediately started screaming and kicking the door to get out. Her brother came running, panicking and trying to get her out, trying so hard to knock down the door and eventually he did.

As soon as she was free they went running round the house frantically looking for their parents, wondering why they hadn't heard their screams. They had disappeared and were nowhere to be found. But where could they be?

Nicola O'Sullivan (15)
St Michael's Catholic High School, Watford

Gone ... ?

I was so glad to be back to school, finally summer was over, and all the nonsense that had happened over summer with the car crash could all be forgotten.

I got up bright and early, and excitedly got ready for school. I felt so grown up, me, Stacy Willis, in Year 10! I picked up my school bag and trotted down the stairs. I headed for the door hearing Mum cluttering around in the kitchen. I called goodbye but she just ignored me. She was crying, she had been crying a lot since the crash, so I just decided to head straight for school.

I got to the road opposite school, I always took great care crossing the road, what with the car crash and all. I felt fairly safe as it was a zebra crossing, I checked both ways and seized my chance to cross, just as I was, a car sped towards me, I hurled myself forward. The car kept on going, it was strange, it was almost as if the car hadn't seen me.

I got into the school gates and saw Sherena walking in front of me with Kelly. She had been with her a lot lately. I was quite cut up about it as Sherena was meant to be my best friend, and Kelly was muscling in trying to take my place. I called Sherena's name but she ignored me and carried on walking, she must have not heard me, no worries, I'd catch her later.

I reached class a bit late as I needed the toilet so I arrived to my form room about 5 minutes after the bell. I walked in but no one looked up. I suppose they were too engrossed in reading. I called out to Miss Cotter that I was sorry for being late, she did not respond so I guessed she just expected me to take my place, as I moved to sit down next to Sherena I noticed Kelly was sitting in my seat. *What is it with that girl, why is she trying to take my place like I'm not here?* Just as I was about to confront her Miss Cotter called out my name, before I could respond, I heard Miss Cotter say, 'Oh Sherena I'm ever so sorry,' and with that Sherena jumped up and made a run for the door. I was just about to run out after her but I was too stunned to move as I realised she had run through me.

A thousand thoughts were running through my head, in the background I could hear wallpaper noise of Miss Cotter saying, 'Sherena is still very upset about the death of Stacey, the car crash really has shaken her up. I guess the office have not got round to taking her name off the register yet ... '

Sapphire Sutton-Clarke (15)
St Michael's Catholic High School, Watford

A Day In The Life Of A Policeman

It is the start of a new shift for the NYPD motorway patrol unit and they are sitting in Doll's Donuts having an early morning break.

Zoom a pick-up goes flying past closely followed by a motorbike which catches the police's attention. 'Go, go, go,' shouts a policeman at the top of his voice. The two tall, slim policemen sprint for their patrol car and follow in close pursuit. The policeman in the passenger seat radios headquarters and wants assistance to arrest the speeding joyriders.

The motorway patrol car has the speeding joyriders in its sight and is closing in on them quicker and quicker. The police helicopter also has the joyriders in their view and are giving information on where the car is to the other patrol cars that are trying to find it.

The speeding young rebels speed under a motorway tunnel causing the police helicopter to lose sight of them but they still have to get rid of the ground units that are on their tail. Now on the outskirts of New York and on the busy motorway with cars and trucks everywhere to be seen the police have to slow down and be extra careful not to crash into any civilians.

The patrol car sirens are blasting to get the civilians to move out of their way so they can keep up with the joyriders. A radio message has come through that spikes have been set out about a mile up the road to stop the joyriders for good.

The joyriders have a trick up their sleeves. One of the joyriders has stolen a police radio and has heard the early warning so they turn off at the next junction just before the spikes. The first set of road spikes have not worked so the police have set up another set on the new road that the rebels have been travelling down. This road is not as busy as the motorway, so the ground units close up the gap and start trying to knock the bike and pick-up off the road for good. The police have just received information the joyriders are wanted in six other states for drug dealing, speeding, failure to stop for police and theft of police equipment. This makes the patrol units even more determined and more willing to catch them as it means a bonus for them.

The police are closing in on the speeding idiots and are getting closer to catching them second by second. Patrol car U102 puts his foot down and goes for the motorbike, that must nearly be out of fuel, it has been going for so long. The patrol car is right up close to the bike and is making the biker panic. The biker, dressed in black leathers, is not concentrating on the road but he is looking at the policeman in his car. A turning in the road is coming up fast and the biker is unaware.

The policeman honks his horn and the biker turns and speeds into the roadside barrier. The radio message is, 'One down, one to go. Good work lads.'

As the police keep on chasing, the pick-up biker is rushed to hospital as it is a horrific accident. The spikes that were set out earlier are coming closer and closer. The pick-up has no idea that they are there, so goes straight over them and immediately loses control and spins out into the trees on the side of the road. The police slam on their brakes and jump out of their cars and run to the crashed car in the trees. The police grab the driver and throws him to the floor. They arrested him and place him in the awaiting cell.

Luke Chambers (15)
St Michael's Catholic High School, Watford

A Day In The Life Of A Cat

I yawn and stretch. I have a lovely soft pink basket. I stand up on my four legs with the intention of begging Bob for some food. I found Bob in the kitchen, his bald head glistening in the morning sun, creeping through the gap in the blinds. He smiles at me and strokes me. He makes those odd noises that humans make.

He puts his jacket on and leaves, but how come he didn't give me any food. Oh yes it will be the diet Jane has put me on. Lucky who can understand human explained what she was talking about.

Ah well there will be food in the bin. I jump up and the bin topples over with a *crash!* I run away terrified under Mary's bed. I hear Jane come downstairs and shout human talk flooding through the house. Mary wakes up, hears me miaowing and picks me up. She cuddles me and gives me a treat. I sneak back to my bed to sleep until teatime.

I wake, the house is silent, it must be early afternoon before Mary and William get home from school. Sure enough I hear feet plodding down the path to the door, it will be ten minutes until Jane gets home, maybe they will feed me. This diet makes me so hungry. Mary sees me and hands me a big bar of Galaxy chocolate, my favourite treat. I bound off to eat it. I go back to sleep after eating it.

Beth Flynn-Jones (13)
St Michael's Catholic High School, Watford

The Sleeping Warriors Of The King

'Tell us a story. Nan, please ...' we begged.

'All right then, which one will it be? The year the lake froze over? The wolf that stole away the sheep? Or even ...' a smile lit up her crinkled face and there was a mischievous glint in her eyes, 'the warriors of King Myrinaz?'

'Who are they?'

'We've never heard that one!'

'Very well. Back in the Old Days, when I was young, there was a battle. A great battle. The greatest one of all. King Myrinaz and his warriors were surrounded by rebel forces, and it looked like all hope was lost. The rebels attacked without mercy, and almost half of Myrinaz's troops were slain in that first charge. But still the survivors fought on. They succeeded in driving the enemy back, beyond the borders of the Realm.

'But that is not the end of the story. According to legend, in times of great need, the brave warriors who died for their king will rise again and come to the aid of the Realm. And indeed, those who remember the Old Days believe that the time has come for the warriors to appear, for these are troubled times. I hope to live to witness that day.

But of course it's just a story,' sighed the old woman. 'It will never really happen ...'

However, she did not know that deep in the Earth, the sleeping warriors were beginning to stir from what had seemed like an endless sleep.

Sophie Devlin (13)
Skipton Girls' High School, Skipton

The Forbidden Miners

2000, an old mine had just been re-built and the miners weren't happy because underground had become a deathbed for workers. Miners were digging themselves a living hell. Manager Tim Olson knew it would be a disaster so he thought that suicide was the answer. The worst damage was occurring down in sector 37, there was no food, water, not even any escape from that crumbly place. The heat was immense down there and there'd already been 14 deaths but still 3 living souls were mining it out for survival, they were doing the impossible to survive, but it seemed too much, all hope was lost. So how did one boy become trapped down this unforgettable death land of ghostly miners?

2007. Fred was lying in the lush green grass at Snaptowns park; this was where Fred took time out from his family, sister and mum. He always came here to think about his dad. His family didn't know this, he just told them he was going to the shop or seeing his friends at the mall.

It was Friday afternoon, he'd been walking for hours just round the town. To the left of him he'd spotted a construction yard with piles of mud stacked up like mountains. There were huge rocks and boulders that had been dug out of the tunnels. A huge sign was wedged in the wet, sloppy mud. Huge dints and splurges of mud were splattered up against it. He could just make out what it said. In huge black bold letters the sign said, *Beware!* Underneath was the small print of writing, 'mining in progress' he stood back and wondered for a minute. Suddenly a man wearing a helmet and orange jacket shouted, 'Hey, what do you think you are doing?' Fred turned to see that he was a worker. Below his collar was a badge with the words, 'Secret Officer'. Next to that must have been his name, some of the letters were missing. 'B ll mi s off' Fred couldn't figure out what his surname was but he knew his first name. The man suddenly approached Fred with an evil eye. As he was about to speak his snake-like tongue seemed to whip across his face. 'Nobody is allowed on these premises without a badge so it's only me, miners and ...' he paused then licked his lips, 'other things.'

Fred was confused, what the hell did he mean about, 'other things'? Fred tried to question him 'What other ... ?'

Then the man stared at him straight in the eye and replied, 'Why would you care?' he leaned forward and faced him just centimetres away from Fred's face. 'You're a kid, you wouldn't know a thing, so remember do not tell anyone you've been here or terrible things will happen to you son, and you wouldn't like that, would you?'

Fred looked to the ground and spoke in a crackling high voice, 'No.'

'Well be off these premises before someone sees you.' And then the man seemed to walk away and vanish behind a digger.

Fred stepped out of the creaky gate and made his way home.

Robert Sparkes (11)
The Kings School, Pontefract

Something Changed

My feet crunched along the thin gravel path towards the large mansion placed in front of me. Every time I looked up the house was becoming clearer and the butterflies in my stomach were gradually getting stronger. My arm was now aching from the heavy bag containing my clothes for the week and of course the old jumper.

They say it's very special to the family, the jumper that is. I don't really know why. I only ever wear it on the rare occasion that I come here, but somehow I just can't get it out of my mind.

My legs were trembling underneath me, my hand shaking as I picked up the heavy door knocker and awaited a reply. Unbelievable, it happened so many years ago and still I'm absolutely terrified. The maid that died, I was there, I saw it. My mind flashed back to that day, a shiver ran down my spine as I remembered all the nightmares I have.

That's why I went back I suppose, to sort it out, to go back to find out there was nothing there. The fact is they don't know what happened, how she got there or why she was there in the first place. All I know is that it was something to do with me.

It doesn't appear to bother my grandparents, I thought, as I heard the door being unlatched; *what do they know that I don't? What is so significant about that old jumper? It doesn't seem that special to me.* The door opened, I cautiously stepped inside not knowing what to expect. I did notice one thing, the atmosphere immediately changed. It was a warm summer's day outside but inside it felt dark, cold and most of all there was an unsafe feeling.

I sat down in the room, the room where I was when it happened. My mind once again flashed back to the very same night. I slowly drank my drink trying desperately to put off thinking about it, but my thoughts just kept returning to the same old jumper.

It was the evening now. It reminded me of the night of the death. The maid had said that a young girl followed her. What scares me the most is the fact that she said the ghost of a young girl was looking for me …

Sophie Mills (12)
The Kings School, Pontefract

The Mask

A giant tiger - like monster, never been seen before strolled through the cities of England at great speed trying to find the mask of power. It was carrying a saw-like disc, retractable knife and a retractable gauntlet. A man stood up to the beast, but the beast whipped out his disc and threw it at the man's head which fell off its body and the disk boomeranged back to the beast. This beast was the solid ghost of a passed away predator. The monster stood at the door of a mansion that recently belonged to a man called Dr Hunt. However, Dr Hunt passed away two months ago and now the mansion is deserted. The beast kicked the door down and inside was an old jumper, a lamp and a portal. The predator dived into the portal and landed on what seemed to be a gravelled path. A few yards up the path was a staircase and so the beast climbed up the stairs and saw the most beautiful thing ever (to it/him) a female predator!

Ben Chappell (12)
The Kings School, Pontefract

The Sleeping Manor

My name is 'Ghost Girl' I am ? years and ? months old. There's nothing much to say about me. When I was alive, I lived with my parents in a grand house with lots of maids and servants, completely surrounded by lime-tree lined boulevards. But all that has changed. Now I float up and down many uneven stairways in a burnt-down wreck that people call 'The Sleeping Manor'. I'm just the kid in the plain brown wrapper, so small no one notices me. No one apart from the boy, way back in the summer of 1743 ...

27th June 1743 by David 12.15pm

It was a sunny day and I was looking out of the window, watching the local kids playing on the grass. My name is David and I live opposite The Sleeping Manor. *Bring bring* That was the doorbell. TJ was coming to call for me. 'Are you comin' out? We could go in The Sleeping Manor! Or are you a scaredy-cat?' he accused.

'Course not!' Well I couldn't let everybody think that, so what else could I say?

'Come on!'

Together we trudged along to the Manor. I could see even TJ looked timid. 'Well go on then, open the door.'

'Erm, er, OK then,' I whispered with extreme care. I twisted the brittle door handle and entered the almost-forbidden house.

Once opened the door swung back to reveal a long gravelled path, a lost highway with signs misleading to nowhere. Hung on the walls, lit lamps, lantern style. At once I reached for the lamp and thrust into the darkness.

'I think we should go back,' I said.

'I agree!' exclaimed TJ. We turned to face a wall. Not a door, just a plain wall, green with the glow of the lamps. 'We're stuck!' yelled TJ. Together we immediately started running into the darkness, only to turn a sharp corner. 'A ghost!' yelled TJ.

1.06pm by Ghost Girl

Together I could see the boys whizzing around the corner. One of the boys skidded on a slightly singed old jumper of mine and dropped their lamp. Once again the house burnt with me inside it! But that didn't matter for I was a ghost already, and already dead. But it was the fact that they saw me that mattered. The fact that another live human being had seen me, a ghost, a spectre, a thing of the past. And in my horror, my guilt of their deaths and my fright, I ran and fled to what used to be the cellars where the servants lived and never came out again.

Hana-Louise Denton **(12)**
The Kings School, Pontefract

My Long-Lost Twin

I walked nervously up the long, winding gravel path. The horrific-looking house in front of me was looking down at me looming closer... My stomach was a fleet of butterflies stampeding like a herd of cows. I knew I should turn around now, but I couldn't! I tried to turn round but my feet had a mind of their own. I started panicking, something was wrong. Very wrong. Then, all of a sudden the sky turned from a nice sunny day to a dark, cold, windy night. The air whipped around my legs causing me to shiver in fright and coldness. I was no more than three metres away from the door when it swung creakily open by itself, then created a loud bang as it hit the stone-crumbling wall.

I came to the door and took a cautious step inside the haunted mansion. Curiously I took a few more steps gazing, peering into the gloom. The door slammed behind me making me jump in fright. Suddenly I heard a noise, it sounded like a young girl screaming. I had made up my mind. I turned around and heaved the old door to look up and found the latch had slid across locking me in. I jumped up at the latch but frustratingly I could not reach, but I had to get out! Somehow! I ran to the room on my left, there was nothing apart from a table containing bread, cheese, a packet of crisps, and a jug of water.

The scream appeared to come from upstairs. It could be my only way out. I took a deep breath and tiptoed as silently as possible up the stairs ...

Jessica Johnson (12)
The Kings School, Pontefract

The Custard Myth

One winter's day a long, long time ago in the small town of Ecelfecon, in Villa 22, lived Mr Edwardo Grammenia. Edwardo was a small fat man with no potential of being a hero of old, or doing anything with his life, at all. He was not good at anything except eating. But for some reason, unknown to me, he got a call to see King Adamus Maxamus. King Adamus wanted to beat Edwardo at a food eating contest to see who had the greater belly. Whoever lost had to venture into the forbidden forest to find the Enchanted Custard. The custard would go to the winner of the food eating contest, to accompany the king's supernatural Flapjack, which had been sent to him from his sister, Fullersena.

Edwardo, as soon as he had got the message, was on his way to see the king: he scurried as fast as he could.

That evening, Edwardo arrived at the palace, he wobbled up to the great table of Choo Shoes and sat on the biggest, grandest, prettiest chair he had ever seen in his life. Then Edwardo realised he was sat in the king's seat and moved as quickly as he could, which wasn't very quick at all.

After getting himself comfy. The king entered in all his glory and wobbled to his seat like a huge jelly. He clapped his hands twice and then as if by magic food was brought in platter by platter, bucket by bucket.

One of the king's men read out the rules of the food eating contest and, '1, 2, 3, go!'

An hour of non-stop eating had passed and they were halfway through their food, the time went on and on, until the king had let out the most gigantic, huge, colossal burp anyone in history had ever let out. The king had won.

The king had all the food taken away with a single clap of his greasy hands. Then he said to Edwardo in a low, gruff, stern voice, 'You, now go and get that Custard for me. I will give you twenty days! Go!'

Edwardo set out on his big adventure to get the Enchanted Custard for the king. He picked the strongest horse he could find and trotted off into the distance.

Sophie Chappel (14)
Vermuyden School, Goole

Sir George And The Cyclops

One strange, mysterious, unusual day, a young handsome knight called Sir George was taking a stroll through the green valley. Sir George was an incredibly strong, brave knight, so heroic and completely fearless, he also had sleek blond hair and sparkly blue eyes. As Sir George walked along the valley, a messenger came charging up and handed Sir George a letter. This letter was from the king asking Sir George to go see him as soon as possible. Sir George didn't know what the king wanted but raced back to the castle to find out anyway.

As he arrived at the castle the king informed Sir George that the most beautiful Princess Bella had been kidnapped by a horrible monster, who was thought to be a Cyclops. The king went on and resulted in setting Sir George the task of rescuing his precious daughter as he was the only one capable of defeating this egregious, human-eating, notorious monster.

A while later Sir George had been home, packed up some food and a couple of daggers, and was now on his journey to save Princess Bella. However, the best way to get to the Cyclops' cave was to go through the deep, dark, haunted forest, but this forest was filled with many dangers as Sir George soon found out. After just three minutes in the forest, Sir George was faced with a fire-breathing dragon. Sir George managed to slay this particular beast with only a slight struggle as it was chained to a tree and Sir George had killed many monsters. Although Sir George had defeated this dragon, he knew pacing through this gloomy wood he would face many other problems before the Cyclops' cave was even in his sight. Sir George had a long, hard journey ahead of him, which would only get worse. This was just the beginning.

Laura Wilson (14)
Vermuyden School, Goole

The Adventures Of Gordon

In the city of Athens, Gordon was on his shift at B & Q when, suddenly out of nowhere, the king's chief messenger stumbled through the door. He had a mission for Gordon which was to slay Fred, the evil black sheep. However this sheep had three heads.

Gordon was already quite famous from when he killed the greedy gnome. He accepted the mission.

He jumped upon the noble flying camel Edgar and left B & Q to visit King Trecious. Trecious and Gordon had been friends for a number of years. But this time he was receiving a royal Bow and Arrow. Gordon left for the field of Fred. There was no farmer as Fred had eaten him. Gordon was almost there, when his sheep bodyguards dropped down from the rooftops. Their poisoned minds only had one thing on the agenda, which was killing Gordon. Gordon drew his sword and killed them one by one, and he only came out with a scratch.

He slowly approached the field of Fred. Suddenly, it went dark, and then he saw the red eyes of Fred opened all six of them. Those brilliant red, evil eyes, so cold yet so bright, then, 'Baa!' Fred bellowed and charged towards Gordon. Urgently Gordon got his bow and shot an arrow, Fred dodged it, but the second shot got him. He cried out and dropped to the ground. Dead. Gordon returned to the Kingdom of Trecious to a hero's welcome. He waited for his next mission.

Paddi McCollum-Nutbrown (14)
Vermuyden School, Goole

Teedius' Nightmare

A few days into the journey he came to a dark, gloomy and rundown forest which was not shown on his map but he had to go through the forest to get where he needed to go. He took a deep breath and said, 'Right let's have it.'

When Teedius was in the depth of the mysterious forest he heard a shallow, light voice saying, 'Get out of this forest or I will harm you beyond belief.' Teedius had heard rumours about a forest that you could hear voices in the shallow breeze, but this did not bother Teedius in the slightest because he had fought bigger and stronger enemies than this. He trampled on, getting deeper into the forest. Things started moving, shadows in the corner of his eyes but by the time he had turned around they were well gone. But then he saw the end of the forest, the light shining through more and more, his pace sped up because nightfall was very soon.

He got out a few minutes before the sun went down and he set up a camp and bed to get some sleep for the defeat of the monster tomorrow.

He was up at the crack of dawn ready to kill the beast which killed children in their sleep. A few hours into the walk he came to the cave of the beast. He lit his torch and started the narrow-pathed descent into the beast's HQ, this path carried on for an eternity but it came to a ginormous room and he could hear the beast's breath rattling off the walls. The beast knew he was here. All of a sudden the beast jumped out and swung for him and he missed by an inch, he swung his sparkling sword at the beast and he hit with pure force, with one slash of the sword the beast was dead.

Matthew Tate (14)
Vermuyden School, Goole

Legend Of Clarkias

The next day Clarkias set off on his fast, trusty, strong steed. Blacky, carrying with him a silver shiny sword, food supplies, such as bread, apples and water, and his gift from the old man.

After travelling through scorching deserts, icy cold glaciers and high, towering mountains, he finally reached the beast's lair, the Dark Forest.

Carefully and cautiously, Clarkias crept into the beast's lair keeping his eyes peeled for any sign of movement.

Suddenly there was a rustling from a clump of nearby bushes. Clarkias sprung round looking for the source of the noise.

The forest was now completely silent of singing birds, as though waiting for a deep plunge.

It all happened so suddenly. From behind the bushes an 8 metre-long, five-headed snake slithered into sight. Clarkias raised his sword as the serpent approached, all heads hissing and waving around in thin air, hoping to scare the beast into retreat. But the serpent just kept on approaching, all the time getting nearer and nearer. Clarkias' feet directed him towards the serpent. Clarkias drew back his sword and slashed viciously at one of the serpent's heads, which fell limply to the ground. Immediately a new head more fierce and vicious than the last sprouted on the severed neck. Clarkias gasped in horror. The serpent swung its massive tail at Clarkias and knocked his sword ten feet away from him. Clarkias pulled out a bag, a gift from the old man, and groped inside it. But to his horror, there was nothing there. He threw it down on the floor in disappointment. A second later something sharp and shiny appeared in the bag. Clarkias swept down to pick it up and found a boomerang with three sharp ends. Using his knowledge of the reappearing heads, Clarkias threw the boomerang at the serpent's body which sliced it in two. Suddenly the two parts of the serpent were eaten up by what appeared to be sparkly crystals.

Beth Mell (14)
Vermuyden School, Goole

Chloe And The Forest

Once upon a time, in a dark, dim and drizzly forest, lived a young girl named Chloe. Chloe was a beautiful, distinguished little girl, who had lived in the forest for many years with her gran.

Even though the forest was a forbidding and threatening place, Chloe and her gran had an amazing home.

However, they were not alone in the forest. At the far end of the woodland lived a hideous, inauspicious, charismatic old man. On many occasions the old man would wreak havoc upon Chloe's gran.

After several months, Chloe decided she had to do something about it. So Chloe set off on her journey across the forest, to the old man's house. On her way, she saw something shining behind a large tree right in the middle of the forest. As Chloe started walking towards the tree she heard steps on the floor like horses' feet rustling leaves. Chloe looked up slowly and saw, standing before her, a beautiful white and pink unicorn.

'Wow!' gasped Chloe. 'What is your name?'

'My name is Glitz,' replied the unicorn.

Chloe and the unicorn were sat talking for hours about how they had never met when they have been living in the same forest for such a long time.

Chloe stood up fast and said, 'Oh no, it is starting to get dark and I need to stop this horrid man who lives across the forest from aggravating my gran.'

'Well jump on my back and we'll fight him together,' said Glitz.

So Chloe and Glitz flew off to find the old man's house …

Chloe Jackson (13)
Vermuyden School, Goole

Knight Of Liberty

Once upon a time, in a small village called Kylan, the king ordered for the Knight of Liberty to come down for a very important meeting. He was recalled as the bravest, most fearless, strongest knight around.

'Good evening, King of Kylan, what was it you wanted to see me for?' insisted the knight.

'Well, I am very unhappy, as the eye-killing dragon has killed all my guards and has taken all of my treasure, that is why I have called you, the Knight of Liberty, to slay the dragon for me, there are just a few things that you will need to do to succeed your brave mission,' explained the king.

'And what will they be?'

Well, you will need to go to the magical wizard of the east; he will have all the things ready that you will need on your journey!'

'OK, my king, away I go to retrieve all of your precious treasure,' announced the knight.

Away the knight went on his fierce journey. He later arrived to the wizard's hut, and was revealed with blacked out glasses, one sword and a shield and some magical sparkle sprinkle juice to rebuild his energy levels up.

'There you are young fellow, take yourself away, and do your king proud. I know he will be pleased.'

'Thank you,' replied the knight.

Later the next day the knight had approached the destination where the dragon awaited the knight.

Suddenly the battle had started, *slice* ... the dragon leapt with pain. The dragon, with its large, yellow, fire-like eyes, directly stared the knight out. The knight only had a matter of minutes left to live, and then he remembered the magical sparkle juice ...

But a blink later the dragon had defeated the knight by its deadly fire-like eyes. The king was furious, that was it, the end of the knight's life.

Leigh Bronnan (13)
Vermuyden School, Goole

The Golden Sword

Once upon a time there lived a magic man named Magico. Magico lived in a dark, dull, frightening cave. No one had visited the cave since 100 years ago. But Magico was afraid of nothing. Although he lived in a cave he had everything he needed and wanted until one day. Magico was bored so he decided to go sit on the edge of a cliff, and just as he was about to sit down he saw the brightest ball of fire above a burning volcano. And in the ball of fire was a bright, golden, shiny sword. *I'm having that,* thought Magico.

So he set out on a tiring, long journey to reach the gold, he crossed hills and deserts and walked through murky waters and over snowy mountains. After this long trip he was exhausted, so he sat down under a tree, and began to fall asleep, but just as he did he was awoken by the blood running down his face. He leapt up and drew out his wand, and stood in front of him was a big brute beast with sharp claws and big green eyes. He pointed his wand at the beast and zapped it into another dimension.

But the journey had to go on to reach the gold so he ran through fields past castles and he was there. A big smile lit up on his face because in front of him was the volcano.

Then the most amazing thing happened. Mr Magico drank a potion he had made earlier and some big white wings grew out of him. He began to fly up the volcano. Finally he reached the top, he walked towards the fire bubble and threw a jug of water over it. And he was just about to grab the sword when a big dragon blocked his path. He drew his wand and said, 'Beast, beast die o die!' And he splattered the beast away. Finally he grabbed the sword and put it into the air and shouted, 'Victory!'

Ryan Watson (14)
Vermuyden School, Goole

William's Quest To Get The Diamond Ring!

It was a dark and gloomy night when a knight called William was riding his horse in a dark forest. When suddenly a man appeared from out of nowhere. The man said to William, 'If you defeat the monster man and get the diamond ring then you will get married to Princess Mary and be the hero of all time.' The man handed a sword and shield to William, 'This is for your protection,' he said.

The next day William was ready for his challenge, to go find the diamond ring. He got on his horse and started galloping through the forest to the cave to defeat the monster man.

William got off his horse and got his sword and shield ready. William saw the monster man and ran to kill him. William stabbed him but the monster man struck back. William got hurt, but carried on, he stabbed him again and the monster man fell to the floor. 'I've done it!' William said proudly, and ran to get the diamond ring.

William was riding back on his horse when suddenly a strange creature jumped out in front of him, then …

Shannon Benton (14)
Vermuyden School, Goole

Mythical Story

One mystical morning, the kingdom, Zig, woke to find their magical and brightly enriched land slowly turning dark, evil and enchanted. The beautiful princess, Lilian Rose, watched in disbelief as her masterpiece fell apart in front of her eyes.

Months passed, many brave, gallant and bold men tried to defeat the evil genius, Zerg Blinfeet. None prevailed. The kingdom slowly kept engulfing in dark, evil and tremendous mystery. One keen and extremely confident man, Slik Terrior, stepped forward and insisted that he would save the kingdom in return of the princess' heart. Lilian Rose accepted the brave man's offer, and off Slik rode into the murky daylight, towards Zerg's evil lair!

Slik battled blistering winds and forceful downfall for many days and nights. One spine-shivering morning, deep in the enchanted land, Slik was faced with a beautiful, unharmed tree. But how could this be? Everything was enchanted by Zerg's evil spell! But this is where three fairies lived. They knew about Slik's quest and knew he needed help. Zara, Tara and Lara flew out towards Slik and granted him with abilities, an invisibility cloak, invincible strength and a helmet of health. Slik was grateful and carried on riding.

It wasn't long till he reached Zerg's lair. Immediately ten million killer fleas struck his body. A fierce battle broke loose! After many back-breaking hours, Slik had defeated the fleas unharmed. Now it was time for Zerg. Slik cautiously crept into the lair, awaiting to be faced with danger! Suddenly, Zerg appeared from the darkness with drool pouring from his mouth, like a tap left running.

Slik struck Zerg's third leg and he collapsed to the floor. Zerg screamed in pain as his heavy load crushed him. Two legs weren't enough to hold his weight. Slik blinded Zerg and rode back to the village. The spell was lifted. The kingdom was turning back.

The kingdom became enriched in flourishing flowers and heart-warming fluffy clouds. Slik had done it! He had lifted the curse! Slik was seen as a local hero and was constantly crowded by people, including the princess, Lilian Rose! Slik had saved the kingdom and won Lilian's heart. Slik was soon knighted Sir Slik Terrior!

Sam Skinner (14)
Vermuyden School, Goole

The Lost Crown

Faraway on an enchanted island, just off South America, lived a beautiful, gorgeous and amazing queen. Unfortunately Queen Beatrice was distressed, due to her crown being stolen. She had no idea what to do. Then one day a knight called Edward the Brave was visiting the magical island. The queen noticed Edward and asked him to retrieve her crown from the derelict castle deep in the enchanted forest, which is where the monster lay waiting.

Edward was a very daring man, he was always prepared for a challenge. So, Edward set off on his journey through the grassy area, weaving in and out of the trees. Then suddenly he noticed a small wooden house in front of him. Edward walked over to the house and knocked at the door. Then the door slowly opened, a puff of smoke appeared with a wizard behind. The tall, thin man handed over a sword and shield and swiftly vanished.

Edward set off back on his journey and finally reached the castle. He walked over to the tall, derelict castle, not knowing what strange creature would be inside. After he had walked over the wooden bridge, he appeared at the door. Edward opened the door with the sword ready in his hand. Then, a gigantic, fat, purple monster came stomping over to Edward. Edward could see the crown twinkling in the background.

Lucy Murphy (13)
Vermuyden School, Goole

The Legend Of Cyprus

Once upon a time, there was a brave, strong, bold man called Cyprus. He travelled far and wide in search for some help as his wife, Elizabeth, had been taken prisoner by the evil giant ogre called Lea. Cyprus travelled far, just to visit his evil brother, Frank.

'What do you want brother?' Frank demanded.

'I want the sword of strength, which will kill the evil, giant ogre, to save my sweet wife!' Cyprus explained.

'Ha! No chance! I don't get what I want, so why should you get what you want?' Frank said, very evilly.

'Frank! She's my wife! Please do something good for a change, and if you do, I will go and get what you want. So what is it you're after? Cypress begged.

'The hand of gold, everything that it touches turns to gold!' Frank shouted.

Cyprus was now on his journey for his evil brother. There it was, right at the top of the tallest mountain, on a dog-like statue. He climbed for days on end and the scenery was absolutely wonderful, it was going on forever but after five days he was finally at the top. He could see the golden hand; all the surroundings were gold. Cyprus climbed to the top of the statue and carefully wrapped it in his cape, and it slowly started turning gold. Suddenly a green monster, covered in orange warts all over, peered over his shoulder. Cyprus spun round, without thinking, touched the monster with the gold hand, and it turned into shiny, glorious gold. Then he threw it in his bag and was on his way back to Frank, to retrieve the sword of strength.

Later, on his way back, he travelled through the dark, haunted forest. Suddenly, there was a strange noise, no ordinary noise. He shivered deeply into his back and bones. Footsteps creaked all around him.

'*Roar!*' it shouted.

The monster couldn't be more better described as a living, walking, so juicy … hot dog. Cyprus ran, as he had no weapons, and all he could think about was how hungry he was.

That's it! he thought.

Cyprus chased after the giant hot dog, and it was stupid enough just to stand there. Cyprus jumped onto the tasty hot dog, with onions and tomato sauce. He began to slowly eat his way through, but by the time he had finished, he was covered in tomato sauce.

Soon, Cyprus was back at his evil brother's house.

'Argh!' Frank screamed, just like a girl.

'What's up Frank?' Cyprus asked.

'B-b-blood!' he screamed again.

'Where? Oh no it's tomato sauce … I had a giant hot dog on my way back, never mind!' he explained.

Cyprus handed over the golden hand to Frank, still wrapped in the scrags of his cape.

'So where is the sword of strength?' he asked.

But there was no answer. Frank had turned into pure, solid gold. That was the end of Frank. Cyprus found the sword of strength behind the chair that Frank was sat in.

Another quest lays for brave Cyprus …

Jamie Tavinder (14)
Vermuyden School, Goole

Pete And The Journey To Treasure

Pete, a strong, brave and kind hero, has a challenge in store for him. There's a box full of treasure in the sea which the king wants desperately but it's not as easy to get as it sounds. As there's a dangerous octopus guarding the treasure, Pete has to secretly go into the sea, grab the treasure and return it to the king. However, if the octopus hears or sees him, he's in big trouble.

As Pete sets off on his long journey to America, which will take at least five days, he can't help but think about how dangerous this could be, but hopefully he will be successful and come home with the treasure.

Five days later and Pete reaches America and is stronger, braver and calmer than ever. When Pete successfully gets the treasure, which he will if he's quiet, everyone will be happy. Pete chucks in the anchor and slowly, safely and quietly gets into the sea with his lucky sword and strong shield. He slowly looks around for the treasure rubbing his eyes. He comes up for a big, deep, long breath and goes straight back under and sees it. He slowly swims to get it. He's doing great!

However, he feels someone patting his shoulder, it's the octopus. Pete is rolled tightly into the octopus' chest. He holds the shield close to him and stabs the octopus. Nothing happens but the octopus goes crazy and Pete escapes.

But what will happen? Who will win?

Cassie Brodigan (14)
Vermuyden School, Goole

The Wand Of Aleria

Once upon a time in an enchanted forest, where nobody dared to go, lived a girl called Olly. Olly, who was a very intelligent girl, was tired of living in the same, boring, dismal forest and longed to be free to roam the land and sights of Crayola.

Olly had lived in the forest all her life, it wasn't all that bad. She learned how to fly on the backs of magical unicorns, to laugh with the giggle fairies, in fact, she had a wonderful life growing up in the forest, but didn't always realise it.

Late one day, when she was cleaning her bunk in the tallest tree of the forest, she noticed something she had never seen before, another little girl. Olly sat and watched the girl playing by a shadowed stream. She wore her hair in bunches, her blonde hair catching the sunlight and gleaming like a star in a summer's night sky. Olly decided she had to get out of the forest and explore these new areas.

The king of the fairies talked to Olly about her escape.

'Make sure you carry the magical wand of Aleria on your travels. You will need this in order to defeat Daisy Dandelion to break free. Good luck.'

Olly rode on the back of a unicorn, took rides across the streams on dolphins, walked the steep, towering, soaring uplands until finally she found her match.

She paced silently towards the first dandelion and took the magical wand out from her belt. Daisy looked down, ready to take a swing at Olly, who was extremely nervous. She squeezed her eyes tightly together and pointed the wand towards Daisy. *Poof!* She was gone. Olly was free.

As she walked out of the enchanted forest, Olly had one last look, took a deep breath and emerged into the world of Crayola.

Ashleigh Marshall (14)
Vermuyden School, Goole

Myths And Legends

Super Saver also known as SS, went to bed one night and awoke the next morning and noticed that his three children had disappeared. He stripped and searched every room in his house, in hope that they would appear, but they were nowhere to be seen. SS looked down and there on the floor was a note. He picked up the note and read out the words: 'I have your children, they are in my cave, if you want to see them alive again, you must bring the king's golden sword, and if you can kill me you can have them back, but if you can't I will eat them alive, you have 72 hours to get here.

Yours faithfully

Bobbobeast'.

When SS had read this note he scurried like a mouse to the king's castle. He told the king what had happened but he forgot to tell him about the note. SS cried out, 'I don't know if I can make it in time.'

Just then the king blurted out, 'Didn't you read the note? You have 72 hours, you have more than enough time. Oh, I mean didn't he or she leave you a note, or anything telling you how and where to find them?'

'How did you know about a note?' SS replied as he slowly stood back up.

'Oh, ur, umm! OK I admit it, I have your children there in the dungeon, I just wanted you to slay Bobbobeast so that I could take the credit for it. I never intended on giving you your children back when you returned, I was going to lock you up with them and use you as servants.'

Just then *bang* the king had hit the floor dead, the priest made Super Saver the king of Hungary. The children ran out of the dungeon and lived happily ever after.

Beth Clarke (14)
Vermuyden School, Goole

Myths And Legends

Firstly, Ellie the fairy has been set the task of finding her father's golden ring. As the ring is precious to her father, he is distressed about the fact that the shiny, unusual, bright golden ring has disappeared.

Ellie the fairy was like an angel; she wouldn't hurt anybody unless they hurt her. She had long blonde hair, wore pretty dresses and carried a magical wand around with her. However, she used it to turn things into something else or to hurt people. It was amazingly powerful.

Because Ellie didn't really know what the golden ring looked like, she had to try and use her magic, her heroic skills and her magical wand to help her find it. Or she risked failing the challenge and losing all her magical powers. Would she want this to happen?

As Ellie set off on her journey, she had a feeling that she would not come back in one piece. 'I have to do this. I do. I have to, come on, I can do it,' she said quietly to herself, as she saw something in front of her.

Because it was a frosty day, she could see two shiny, slithering snakes approaching her. Ellie got very scared, terrified and fearful. As she winced at the beastly snakes, which had green, orange and black stripes, she noticed they had four eyes and three arms protruding from their muscular bodies.

Courageously Ellie grabbed her sword from her side and pointed it at them threateningly. They came face to face. As the scariest snake made the first move, spitting at her fiercely, she chopped off its head. Surprisingly the vicious snake grabbed her hand, so she stabbed it in the back. They were laid there as if they had been shot by lightning.

Because they were dead, Ellie could see the golden ring behind them so she went to reach it, but all of a sudden …

Amie Rothery (14)
Vermuyden School, Goole

Myths And Legends

Once upon a time there was a great and fearless warrior called Lisa the Great. Fearlessly she had to go on a very long and tireless journey to the evil queen Victoria's castle, to claim the golden crown. Desperately, she needed the golden crown to help set her father free from prison.

Lisa set off on her journey towards the Queen Victoria's castle. She had to go over rocky mountains and slippery slopes, on her horse Beauty. It was a very long and tiring journey for both Lisa and her horse. However her journey was not at all simple like she had first thought. On her way, she saw what looked like a man. As she got closer, she realised it was half man half spider: the queen's most loyal bodyguard. Knowing that she could not defeat it with the minute, blunt sword that she had, she turned around and galloped away as fast as she could.

Lisa went to see a very old but magical wizard, called Albutt the Great, who gave her the sword of all magical powers. Now Lisa had the magical sword, she set off on her journey again. As she ventured over rocky mountains and slippery slopes, towards the queen's castle, she began to feel the magical powers taking over her.

She defeated the half man half spider monster and went straight into the queen's castle. The queen had been waiting for Lisa and they started to battle fiercely. Within minutes, the queen was dead and Lisa had the legendary golden crown. She took it down to the prison and swapped it for her father. Now Lisa and her father are to become king and queen.

Lisa Siddons (14)
Vermuyden School, Goole

Alex The Warrior

One bright, happy, sunny day in a small town, there was a hero called Alex the Warrior. He was set a difficult, hard challenge, to get a ruby diamond by King Edward. The sparkly, magical, red diamond was hidden well into the dark, gloomy and creepy forest.

As Alex set off with his white horse, sharp, glistening sword and metal shield, he went over bridges, then he came to the entry of the dark forest. Through muddy lakes, past golden beaches and sunsets.

Alex got off his horse and bravely entered the wood, unaware of what was in the wood, he slowly walked into the forest, looking back at his horse all the time ...

'Oh, my, I am sorry dear chap,' said a tall, young leafy tree.

'It's OK,' replied Alex.

'I never normally see people here, this is the dark forest, very scary I must say,' said the tree.

'Well my name's Woody.'

'Nice to meet you Woody!'

'Do you know where I could find a ruby diamond? asked Alex.

'Well,' said Woody, 'nice to meet you, Woody.'

'Do you know where I could find a ruby diamond?' asked Alex.

'Well ... in fact, Woody, you could try the big tree, in the centre of the wood, but be carefully, I've heard that's a nasty tree and he hasn't been woken for years.

OK well thank you anyway and goodbye,' said Alex happily.

So, Alex set off looking for a big tree in the centre of the wood. Alex had been gone for a few hours when he finally found a massive tree, with a beam of light shining on it. Alex slowly walked up and saw a glimpse of red,

Alex went to grab when ... the big scary tree started moving. 'How dare you disturb me from my sleep!'

So Alex quickly got out his sword, *swosh!* Alex grabbed the ruby and ran ...

Melissa Usher (14) & Chloe Johnson
Vermuyden School, Goole

The Lost Heirloom

A knight was walking through the forgotten forest and, after a few hours, a city appeared before him. He journeyed down the grassy hills of Tamriel, went towards the city guard and asked him, 'What city is this, may I ask?'

'Why Sir, it is the imperial city, say, you look like a knight who can fight off a few creatures. Would you? The Emperor in the palace is in need of help.'

So, the knight went to the palace and asked to talk with the Emperor about something he needed help with. The well-protected palace guard went in to see if the Emperor wanted to speak with the knight. 'Thank the gods someone has come to help me!'

They started talking and the Emperor explained that he had recently found out his family had lost an heirloom, which was an enchanted Amulet and was hidden in the north-western mountains. He kindly asked the knight to retrieve it for a handsome reward of 6,000 pieces of gold.

When the knight was on his quest, he stumbled across a very old vampire. At first he was going to attack but he stepped back in fear of the knight. As he stepped back he kept talking to the knight as though he was talking to himself. However, he informed the knight what would happen in his quest and that he should remain cautious in the Amelion Tomb. But … would he take notice of this vampire … ?

Michael Bailey (14)
Vermuyden School, Goole

Sir Tristan And The Princess

Ever since he was a little boy, Tristan had wanted to become a knight, because only knights and princes were allowed to marry the beautiful princess Tara. The king knew that this was why he wanted to become a knight, and decided that since Tristan was so honest, loyal and brave, he would become a knight. This is who he wanted his daughter to marry. Tristan's enemy Hagan, however, had been trying to win Princess Tara's heart for a long time. When he heard the news, he set about making a plan. He asked his mother Ethel, a dark witch, to help him.

The knighting ceremony was a bright and exciting occasion, the grand hall of the king's palace was elaborately decorated, and there was an orchestra providing entertainment. The king was wearing his best robes, and each of his three daughters had made a special effort, but Tara looked the most stunning and graceful, and Tristan couldn't keep his eyes off her. The ceremony started and everyone took their seats and Tristan knelt before the king with his head bowed.

Just as the king pronounced him Sir Tristan, Ethel flew in a typhoon of wind and smoke, and snatched Tara up. Tara struggled to get away but it was useless in Ethel's iron grip. Ethel laughed a cruel cackle and screeched, 'She's mine now; you'll never get her back!' and with that she was gone. The king was distraught; he ate little and slept less, constantly worried about the safety of his beautiful daughter Tara. For the past week, Tristan had asked every day if he could go after her, and every day he had said no. Plenty of other knights had gone, but none had returned. But on the Sunday that marked exactly one week since Tara had been taken, his desperation forced him to say yes.

Jessica Driver (14)
Vermuyden School, Goole

The Curse Of Ledso

Heroically, the valiant knight raised his gargantuan silver axe and hacked at the almighty dragon of Grimweld. The dragon let out a desperate cry before it plunged into the pit of destruction. It was over, finally over. The knight fell to his knees. Once again he had saved his village from the clutches of evil.

The following day he was paraded through the long, cobbled, winding streets of Ledso common. The throng chanting the name 'Auron.' It was the day of dreams. Suddenly the celebrations turned to screams, the delirium turned to dismay. People were elevated into the air, desperate for air. Above the pandemonium, a dark silhouette rose. 'I am your new master,' croaked the hooded figure. 'I am the Nebron Mage.'

For the years that followed that tragic day. The mage was the dictator of all evil. The forceful presence, which was Auron, had perished at the hands of him. Little did he know, a new hero was being trained, his name was Strife. He was the burliest and most skilled swordsman the world had ever seen.

'You are practically ready young master,' wheezed swordsmaster Sephiroth. 'One last test; you must claim the life of your mentor.'

'What!' spluttered Strife. 'But you are like the father I have never had, I won't do it.'

'You must make sacrifices to achieve your destiny.'

And with one final swipe of his sword he decapitated his teacher, his friend, his father. He fell to his knees.

Adam Hewson (13)
Vermuyden School, Goole

Percy And His Journey To America

Percy, a hero, was a kind, helpful, considerate guy. He came across a problem that he had to get over to America to get the gold ring that was going to help him propose to Princess Sophie. Percy wanted to marry Sophie so, so, so much that he decided to go over to America for the ring. Princess Sophie was a polite, wealthy and caring girl. Everybody loved her, especially Percy! She had lovely long blonde hair and sparkling blue eyes.

As Percy set off on his journey to America, he didn't realise how long it was going to take him to reach it. It was going to take at least up to three days because he was travelling on his tall, brown and timid horse. Percy turned around and saw a weird creature following him. He was scared, worried and panicking. The creature kept shouting, 'Oi you come here,' but Percy kept on travelling. Finally the creature reached Percy, jumped up and kissed him on the cheek then ran off! Percy laughed. Percy saw a shed in the middle of a field with the door open, he went over to see and there were two swords there. Percy picked them up and took them with him.

Percy and his horse galloped across to the field where he was told the ring would be. From the distance they were they could see something stood still like a statue. They trotted over and Percy saw some kind of villain, he jumped off the horse and explained everything to the villain, but the villain didn't understand a word! Percy reached his hand over to reach the box with the ring in, but the villain gave a quick push.

What happened next? Did Percy marry Sophie?

Jessica Brown (14)
Vermuyden School, Goole

Steveias And The Dragon!

One day Steveias went to King Rich to collect some treasure and the £100 million platinum ball. He arrived at the castle, and it was gloomy, dark and creepy. Steveias crept inside so he didn't make too much noise. King Rich was sat in his throne sleeping. Steveias accidentally knocked over a metal jug of water. King Rich awoke quickly. 'Who is there, may I ask?'

Steveias replied proudly. 'It is I, the dragon slayer! I am here to get the £100 million platinum ball and I'm here to see your daughter Princess Vickeh as she sent me a letter saying she needed my help.'

Then King Rich lowered his voice and said, 'My daughter needs a husband, she needs to take the royalty into her own hands and she needs responsibility, she loves you ...'

Steveias was shocked to realise such a beautiful girl liked him, he blushed and said, 'OK, I'm ready to get the £100 million platinum ball and to love your daughter!'

King Rich told Steveias to take some weapons to defeat James the dragon.

He told the king, 'I am strong, I'm undefeatable, and I'm willing. I need to do this alone or I won't feel the same precious feeling.'

At that moment King Rich yelled, 'Set off now! It's time!'

Steveias jumped out of his skin, got on his golden horse and rode off, he got to a kingdom called Vesuvius.

When Steveias arrived he sat down next to a tree, he took a mouthful of water from the nearby clear valley and pulled out some cherrie-crunch-popsic-tastic-beans out of his bag which he carried everywhere, as he crunched away on his beans he heard a voice from up above. 'Excuse me, but could you please stop crunching loudly and get off my roots!'

Steveias dropped everything, he circled the tree many times, the tree yelled, 'Please stop! I feel dizzy! I'm Paul, please don't hurt me! I've heard all about you but I'm here to help you, I can help you kill James the dragon.'

Victoria Hanlon (13)
Vermuyden School, Goole